The Overseas Nanny Mistake

by Rebecca Hunter

THE OVERSEAS NANNY MISTAKE

ISBN: 978-1-958376-50-8

Cover Design by Kelsey Bowman, Let's Get Lit Design Studio

The Overseas Nanny Mistake takes inspiration from *Jane Eyre* by Charlotte Bronte and *Rebecca* by Daphne du Maurier, but you don't have to have read either book to enjoy Edward and Ava's story. If you love mysterious manor houses, brooding heroes and intrepid heroines, this book is for you! Welcome to the Vallenberg estate…

Chapter 1

I think I forgot my phone charger. I brought the adapter for Swedish plugs and the voltage converter so my phone wouldn't explode or whatever happens when you get that wrong, but the actual charger? It was still plugged into the wall in my bedroom back in Brooklyn. To be fair, when I scanned the room one last time, I thought it was my niece Daisy's, which is the kind of thing that can happen when your bed is only a few feet away from someone else's.

Still, my only tie to home was going to die in sixteen percent of something. As the taxi followed the curvy road through the pine forest, I rummaged through my oversized handbag, pushing aside my favorite red lipstick I'd reapplied in the airport bathroom, my toothbrush case and toothpaste, which I'd also used in said bathroom, and the box of condoms I was determined to break open at some point this summer. The bottom of my bag was in view, and my phone charger definitely wasn't there.

Don't panic. I could just buy a new cord…somewhere. Outside the window was the winding, two-lane road and trees. Lots and lots of trees. We had passed the last signs of Stockholm a while ago, but there must be stores around here. Or maybe this mysterious family I'd be nannying for would have an extra cord?

The taxi followed a short curve, then turned in to a gravel driveway marked by two moss-covered stone pillars, one on each side, and a wrought-iron gate. When the taxi came to a stop, the driver turned in her seat to face me.

"Are you sure this is the right place?"

I checked the address one more time, ignoring another low battery warning, then looked up at the tarnished bronze plaque on the right pillar for confirmation.

"Yes," I said, though I sounded more confident than I felt.

The woman gave a little shrug, then got out of the car to open the gates. Metal scraped on metal as the hinges creaked open. We continued, making our way through the forest, around flat stone hills and clumps of pines. Thick clouds above cast dark shadows on the ground. As we rounded an enormous boulder, the forest opened, and there it was. My breath caught in my throat as I stared out the taxi window. In front of me was a manor, not a house.

Long, elegant pairs of windows lined the first floor, and there were more on the second, along with balconies with thick, columned railings. The windows on the third story were smaller, in narrow dormers that poked out of the copper roof, tinted green by the elements. Roses on bushy vines were trained up the wall and over the first-story windows. They clung to the second-floor balcony, and they hung over the entranceway. The place would have been unbearably ostentatious if it didn't look so much like a crumbling relic. It was the kind of manor house that reeked of generations of money, of families clinging to their past.

This was my home for the next eight weeks?

The taxi started around the circular driveway, passing a row of garages, and came to a stop in front of the main entrance to the house. The driver turned off the engine, then glanced over her shoulder. "Nice place."

I gave a little snort at her understatement. I smoothed out the wrinkles in my dress, trying to hide the just-slept-in-this look. A glimpse at my hair in the window's reflection showed brown frizz escaping the ponytail I'd fastened at the airport. My mother's voice rang in my ears: *Make sure you look presentable.* I smoothed my hair, then opened the car door. The humid air poured in, filled with the damp, verdant scent of grass and roses. I closed my eyes for a deep breath, then stepped out onto the gravel path. This was way too good to be real.

The driver set my luggage on the gravel driveway. "Do you want me to wait here until you get in?"

"No thanks," I said quickly.

She gave me a dubious glance and handed me her card. "If you change your mind, please call."

She climbed back into the taxi and drove away, leaving me alone in front of my new summer home. I grabbed my luggage and walked up the path, the gravel crunching under my feet. The grass was a deep green, the kind that suggested plenty of rain, and it seemed to glow under the heavy grey clouds that covered the sky. In front of me was an archway, and beyond that, a thick, wooden door with a brass knocker at its center.

I took a deep breath, trying to calm the heavy thump of my heart. Was this a dream? Maybe I had fallen asleep on the plane and hadn't woken yet. Except the scents were too foreign, and this manor house was too far from what my Brooklyn-born mind could come up with. I'd never smelled roses like this, out in the wild, mingling with grass and other scents I couldn't identify. It was as if those years of reading lush, historical romances had paid off. All those years of imagining and wanting and longing were no longer just dreams.

The closer I came to the door, the more I noticed how quiet it was. No din of traffic, no hum of voices, just the chirps and twitters from the surrounding forest. I took a steadying breath and found the doorbell. There was a faint, stately chime from inside. I straightened up and waited.

When I filled out my application at Practically Perfect Nannies, they asked the usual questions about qualifications—mine consisted of an almost-finished degree in psychology, two summer nannying jobs in New York, and raising my niece while my sister Brenda and her married boyfriend Donny…didn't. They also asked how far I was willing to travel. That was easy. I wrote that I'd like the farthest assignment from my family's three-bedroom apartment in Brooklyn. As someone who'd never been outside the Tri-State Area, I'd imagined it would take me somewhere distant and quaint like Vermont or even Maine. Instead, they offered me Stockholm.

"But I don't speak Swedish," I'd said to Miriam, the woman who interviewed me.

"That's exactly what the client wants. Their daughter understands English."

In my mind, Manhattan was far from home. I'd never been on an airplane, let alone one that took me to another country. I was about to say as much, but Miriam added, "The house is right on the Baltic Sea, and you'll have your own suite, with a bedroom and a bathroom."

And just like that, all my hesitations disappeared. I pictured myself in my very own room, with the door closed, taking leisurely showers every night because no one else needed to use the bathroom. I knew I should be dreaming a little bigger, but sharing an apartment with four-and-a-half people doesn't make you think rationally about this kind of thing.

"They've also offered a bonus," she continued. "One thousand dollars for every week you stay."

My eyes probably widened because she added, "That usually happens when something about the situation is…challenging."

But I was already sold on my own suite.

The agency had given me very little information about the family I'd be working for, which I found strange considering the number of pages of the NDA I'd signed. I was working with six-year-old Sofia Vallenberg, daughter of Edward and Rebecca…and that's pretty much all I knew. The couple hadn't listed their occupations, nor any of the other usual details you'd find.

I turned to the internet and found a few photos of the couple at a black-tie event back in New York. Rebecca was blond and elegant, with a willowy figure that was the polar opposite of mine. Her smile was lovely but reserved, while Edward didn't smile at all. His dark hair was neatly combed, and his deep blue eyes were piercing. His tuxedo fit perfectly, which I guess was to be expected of a man who owned a house like this. He had the kind of broodingly good looks that made me remind myself that he was married. I had a knack for falling for authority figures, but thinking of my sister's ongoing affair with a married man usually worked to kill that attraction.

Most of the information about the Vallenbergs was in Swedish, of course, and a quick translation attempt was enough of a word salad for me to give up my investigation. There were a few words that popped up in titles, like *skandal*...which looked a lot like *scandal*. I couldn't find anything in English about it, so I gave up and decided to leave the rest to fate.

I waited outside the door. One minute. Two. I couldn't hear any movement, so I tried again, ringing the doorbell, then used the heavy knocker for good measure. Still nothing. I pulled out my phone and looked up the number for Practically Perfect Nannies. It was 11:30 a.m. in Stockholm, which was 5:30 a.m. in New York. A little early to call. My phone was now down to ten percent, which seemed like a precipitous slide since the last time I'd looked, so I powered it off for emergencies.

"Hello? Is anyone there?"

The long overnight flight plus the intoxicating scent of the roses and the dewy forest were conspiring to put me to sleep. If no one was here, maybe I'd curl up in the gazebo I'd spotted around the side and take a nap. It wouldn't be the best first impression if they discovered me, but then again, neither was leaving home when your new nanny was supposed to—

The door creaked open.

"Hello, I'm..." The words died in my throat as I took in the man standing in the doorway. Edward

Vallenberg was taller than I'd imagined from the photographs, built with wide shoulders and a tapered waist in a way that made me notice. Today he had on a crumpled collared shirt, unbuttoned at the sleeves, and his grey wool slacks didn't look any better. His hair was a bit on the long side, with a hint of a curl that gave a softer look to his chiseled jaw and pronounced cheekbones. His hair was also a tousled mess, like he'd slept on it, then ran his hand through it too many times. His eyes were the blue of the sky when the sun set, dark and rich, and under dark lashes I could see faint circles, like he hadn't slept well. And still, I was captivated. My heart raced, the combination of excitement, nerves, and exhaustion pumping through me. His gaze was intense, so I looked at his mouth instead, with plush lips that were making me think about the last thing I should, especially since his expression was anything but welcoming. *Displeased* was the best word for the hint of a frown I detected.

"You are…?" he prompted.

"I'm Ava Martello?" Somehow, I made my name sound like a question. This didn't seem to clear up anything for him, so I added, "Your new nanny? From Practically Perfect Nannies in New York?"

My voice was too chipper, like some sort of insecure Mary Poppins. Was this going to be a worse first nanny impression than sleeping in his gazebo? I took a deep breath and stood taller, and his eyes raked up and down my body like he was assessing me. His expression was blank, impersonal, but it left a trail of heat that ran through my body.

Married, I reminded myself.

"Today's the twenty-third, correct?" He had an upper-crust British accent, perfectly enunciated, a contrast to the husky tones of his voice.

"Yes, it is."

My heartbeat kicked up as he frowned down at me, his blue eyes guarded and impenetrable. "What are you doing here?"

I stared at him, my inappropriate thoughts leaving my brain as I registered the look on his face. He looked confused and vaguely irritated. What the heck was going on? He'd given a slight nod when I'd mentioned Practically Perfect Nannies…

"You hired me as your nanny, remember?"

"But my assistant changed your arrival date to the thirtieth."

What?

"Um…I didn't get that message, and neither did the agency, as far as I know." I'd talked to Miriam yesterday before I left to confirm all the details.

The lines on his forehead deepened, and he continued looking at me as if this was my mistake, not his. "Is this some kind of scam?"

"What do you mean?"

"Showing up at my doorstep…" He broke off the sentence, and I raised my eyebrows, waiting for him to continue. Now I had no idea what he was talking about.

"You just look so…" He gestured up and down the length of me. Unwelcome heat slipped under my skin, tingling, spreading further. He frowned. "Never mind."

Now I was irritated. "Of course this isn't a scam. You got a photo of me with all the documents I sent."

"My assistant takes care of the logistics."

I resisted an eye roll. "Let me show you the message and my contract."

My face heated as I rummaged through my bag for my phone, resigned to using some of my remaining battery power on this issue. Damn. I'd wanted to make a good impression so badly, and this was pretty much the opposite. I fumbled with my phone and powered it back on.

"Here it is," I said, tapping on my latest email from Practically Perfect Nannies, confirming my scheduled arrival. I noted that Miriam had cc'd a woman I assumed was his assistant, but not Edward.

Edward reached for my phone and stared at it. His biceps stretched against the material of his shirt, which I tried really hard not to focus on. How can you be both irritated and turned on by a guy at the same time? It seemed a little counterproductive, evolution-wise.

Finally, he let out a sigh. "Come in. There's something we need to discuss."

I took that as a step in the right direction, albeit a small one. He held open the door, and I rolled my clunky suitcase through the opening. My eyes strained in the dark entryway as the door closed behind me. Edward flipped on the light switch, and a chandelier hanging high above lit the space. I was very, very aware of how quiet it was, like no one else was in this enormous place. I was also very, very aware of how close he was. Every inch of my skin tingled with that awareness. Where were his wife and daughter? And where was the butler…or whoever handled everyday living for him? There was no way this family cooked and cleaned for themselves.

"You can wait in the living room," he grumbled, gesturing down the hallway. "I'll return in a moment."

He disappeared into a room off the side, leaving me alone in his entryway. I abandoned my suitcase by the door and made my way down the hall. It had an old-fashioned elegance that made me want to explore, like it was the kind of place where some magical fantasy story might happen. The walls were papered in deep red silk with plaster flourishes and elegant moldings around the sides, and the doors had fussy brass handles. The floor was wood, old but well preserved, and it creaked under my feet like I'd imagine a haunted house might.

I followed the Persian runner into what looked like a living room. The room had the same European-old feel as the hallway, with high ceilings and pairs of long windows that opened out onto a stone patio. In the near corner there was a tile stove-like thing that was definitely old, too, and from the ceiling hung another glassy chandelier. The furniture was sparse, as if someone had removed half of it while this guy was sleeping, but the pieces looked newer, classy, and expensive: a sofa, a coffee table, and one lonely armchair.

The most surprising thing was the mess. The leather sofa was an ocean of abandoned stuffed animals and dress-up clothes, and kids' books were piled in a tottering heap on the floor next to it. Dirty plates and glasses were carelessly left on the coffee table, and I could practically hear my mother's voice from across the ocean, calling, "Use a coaster." Housekeeping hadn't been mentioned as one of my duties, but I was starting to feel like I should volunteer my services. It was one of those quirks of living in a crowded three-bedroom apartment: I needed a clean environment.

Only the armchair was free of clutter. It was stately, made of soft-looking brown leather, the kind where you wanted to curl up and read a book while it rained.

I'd always felt like families were the best kind of mysteries, complicated and intriguing messes of conflicting hopes, loyalties, fears, and disappointments. As I scanned this room, I had no idea what to make of this family.

I started for the armchair, just to try it out. I was almost sure it was Edward's. If he came in while I was in his chair, would he ask me to move? Or would he sit among the stuffed animals? Neither seemed like a good option, so I headed for the sofa. I pushed aside a stuffed octopus and an oversize dog and sat, smoothing the hem of my skirt so it came closer to covering my bare knees.

From somewhere close by, the melodious tones of Edward's voice in Swedish floated in, but there was no answer, like he was on the phone. I tried to think about anything else except how much I loved his voice, the rough grumble in that highbrow British accent…

I had this thing about falling in love with authority figures. My first was Matteo Romano, my boss at Caffe Roma back when I was seventeen, and my most recent obsession was Dr. Benjamin Chu, my developmental psych professor my sophomore year. After three years of scouring the Hunter College catalog for another class I could take with him, my best friend Ruthie tried to talk some sense into me. But I couldn't help it. After a while of doing what these men asked, of trying to please them, it turned into this sexual dynamic for me.

Not that anything sexual ever happened, just as Ruthie had promised. Brenda's theory was that I was self-defeating, falling for men I couldn't have, because I was too shy to meet anyone real. I thought that was rich coming from someone dating a married man. Ruthie said I wanted someone who would take care of me, which made sense considering the number of responsibilities that ended up on my shoulders. I didn't think it mattered too much why I kept falling for authority figures, just that I liked it, but I had to agree with both Brenda and Ruthie: I needed to find someone who wasn't my professor or my boss so I could finally have sex with someone…or at least go out on a date or two. I'd managed to make it through two nanny jobs without falling for my boss, which was why this job was perfect. This summer was supposed to be a three-birds-with-one-stone thing: move out of my family's apartment, get paid to hang out in a foreign country with a kid, and have a fling with someone who was *not* my boss. I still hadn't figured out how to casually bring up my virginity during this hypothetical fling, but I could worry about that part later.

Edward appeared in the doorway before I could rid myself of that thought. His hair was a little less messy, at least in the front, like he'd made a halfhearted attempt to get it to lie flatter. He crossed the room and settled into the brown chair, looking perfectly at home in it. He leaned forward, his elbows on his knees, his legs wide in that confident way that men had when they're used to taking up space in the world. I reminded myself to keep my eyes on his face.

"There's been a mistake," he said. "My secretary confirmed that the change of dates didn't go through."

I blinked at him. "What kind of mistake?"

"I don't need a nanny until next week."

"Next week?" I echoed.

Of all the scenarios I'd imagined since I'd taken this job, this definitely was not one of them.

"My daughter isn't here."

I glanced down at the stuffed animals surrounding me on the sofa. "Really?"

He looked at them too, and his expression softened. That moment was like a window into a totally different side of this grumpy, irritated man, but before I could interpret the look, it faded.

"I'll make arrangements for you to go back home," he said brusquely.

Go back home? He was going to send me back to the tiny three-bedroom apartment, to my life that I had finally found a way to break free of?

"I can't go home," I said too quickly to hide the panic in my voice.

He frowned. "Are you in some sort of trouble?"

There was concern in his question but also a hint of suspicion. Not that I blamed him. I mean, I wouldn't want my nanny to be dodging trouble either.

"Nothing like that. It's just…" I bit my lip, trying to figure out a way to sum up my nutty family. If I went back to New York, I knew something would go wrong, something that would keep me from coming to Stockholm again. I had barely escaped. Last summer, just before I was supposed to start my junior year at Hunter College, my sister roped me into staying with my niece while she went to New Jersey with her married boyfriend, and she didn't come back until two weeks into the fall semester, which meant I was juggling taking my niece to school and getting to my own classes. Family crises over the years had left me dropping enough credits to turn a four-year degree into six. If I returned, Brenda would need me, and I wouldn't be able to say no—not when Daisy was concerned.

But anything I said to Edward on the subject might make him less inclined to let me stay. He was still waiting for me to answer, his eyes fixed on me in a way that made me think about all the things I shouldn't.

"It's just that I gave up my living situation," I said. That wasn't quite a lie. I had given up living with my family, as in, I'd sworn to myself that I'd never do it again.

"You have nowhere to go?"

"I wouldn't be homeless, if that's what you're asking, but…it wouldn't be ideal."

Edward nodded, seeming to accept this explanation. "So you want me to let you stay here?"

He raised his eyebrows and gestured around the messy room. That gave me an idea.

"I can be your temporary housecleaner," I said brightly. "I'll straighten up and clean and organize or whatever you'd like. I can make you dinner…"

My voice trailed off as I noticed his eyes were no longer on my face. They were on my hands, still smoothing my skirt. I could have sworn that a dark flash of desire swept over his face, but the look disappeared so quickly that I wasn't sure if I'd imagined it.

His gaze snapped back up to mine, and he shook his head.

"I already have a housekeeper," he grumbled.

I eyed the stuffed animals and the empty glasses and plates on the coffee table in front of me. We both knew how ridiculous that statement sounded.

"I gave the staff a few weeks off, so it's a bit of a mess," he conceded. He paused, his long fingers tapping on the leather armrest. "This is not what I planned."

"Me neither," I said dryly before I thought better of it.

He raised his eyebrows, and my cheeks heated up. I bit my lip and decided to give him a moment to think about it. I knew the reasons I shouldn't be here right now, alone with a very attractive man who was also my boss, but that problem would be solved as soon as his wife came home. Why was he hesitating?

The storm clouds that had threatened since I'd landed finally made good on their promise. Rain began to fall, first in light taps, then in a quicker staccato. In the distance, thunder rumbled. Heavier drops hit the window, and we both turned to watch them. He wouldn't kick me out in the middle of a thunderstorm…would he?

As if he'd heard my thoughts, Edward said, "Well, I'm not going to send you out in the rain."

He said it in a way that suggested he'd considered it.

"I could start cleaning now, just while it rains," I said, my voice upbeat and hopeful. *We can make this work.* "Maybe just until your wife comes home? You could discuss it with her and let me know?"

His face darkened. "There is no wife coming home."

I'd been wrong when I'd thought he was scowling before. When the word *wife* came out of his mouth, his eyes narrowed with anger and bitterness.

"Oh." My voice was barely a whisper. Suddenly everything made sense. The messy, silent house. His insistence that I leave. If he let me stay, it would just be him and me. My *boss* and me. My ultimate kryptonite. *Oh.*

How did this happen? Both parents were listed on the client form, and this was the only address I'd been given, but I guess that didn't mean they were together. All the carefully posed photos I'd seen in my search showed them together, but those must have been a couple of years old.

We both looked back at the rain. It was blowing hard against the glass now, turning the grey stone patio and the green expanse of lawn beyond it into a muted blur. I shifted, the smooth leather cool under my bare legs. My best strategy was probably to be as quiet as possible in hopes of convincing him that he wouldn't notice me if I was here. A bolt of lightning flashed, and thunder cracked, echoing through the room. I jumped in my seat, clutching the stuffed octopus next to me. Which probably wasn't a good look. Okay, forget waiting in silence.

"I'll do some tidying up this afternoon while we figure this out," I said, my voice chipper. He didn't say no to that, so I continued. "Just this room. I won't bother you."

He opened his mouth like he was getting ready to speak, but decided against it. He ran his hand through his hair, ruining all the progress he'd made to tame it.

"Let me make a couple of calls," he said, standing. "The cleanup really isn't necessary."

"Honestly, I really prefer it that way." This was completely true. Messy rooms like this made me squirm. Plus, there was no way I could sit back and do nothing this afternoon while he decided my fate. I gave him a smile that I hoped said, *you'll like this. You'll like me.*

He shrugged, apparently unmoved. "Suit yourself."

"Thank you," I said, even though it was a little absurd that I was thanking him for the chance to clean his house. But I figured it wouldn't hurt my case.

He nodded and turned down the long hallway, leaving me alone.

If I were the kind of person who could afford a therapist, they would probably trace my need to please everyone back to my family, the need to transcend the chaos and not let it define me. I spent a lot of my teens smoothing out all the ripples, waves, and occasional tsunamis my sister caused or picking up my mother's building maintenance work when she was too tired from her nannying job. But I didn't have enough money to move into my own apartment, let alone pay for a therapist. I had the second-best thing, Ruthie. And I knew what she'd say about my current situation. "Do whatever it takes to get your way."

In my case, that meant pleasing my new, buttoned-up boss, while avoiding the disastrous kind of crush that had wreaked havoc the last two times. Which meant avoiding situations that my brain could sexualize. It was a surprisingly creative brain in that respect.

But I was organizing his living room. He was a fool if that didn't please him.

Chapter 2

Despite my exhaustion from my mostly sleepless overnight flight, I got to work, partly so I wouldn't nod off on Edward's sofa and partly so I had something else to think about besides my inappropriate boss preoccupations and the impending decision said boss was about to make about staying here.

I started by stacking the dirty glasses and plates from the coffee table to take them to the kitchen—except I didn't know where the kitchen was. Edward hadn't shown me around or even pointed me toward a bathroom. I wandered back into the dark hallway, past closed doors, and headed for the first open doorway. My heart raced as I came to the corner, like Edward might catch me with his stern, brooding stare…

I pushed away that thought and walked into a formal dining room. In the center was a heavy wooden table on a red-and-white Persian rug, surrounded by tall-backed chairs with seats upholstered in more red silk. There was a door on the opposite side of the room. Did it lead to the kitchen?

Balancing the dishes in one hand, I pushed it open, taking in the room. It was, in fact, the kitchen, and it had that same old-fashioned feel to it, with a tall ceiling and a wood floor. The counters and backsplashes were covered in hand-painted, blue-and-white tiles, with matching designs on the white, wooden cabinets, but the appliances were all modern, in shiny stainless steel. Somehow, it managed to work. In the corner of the room—and the house—was a long, wooden table, and above the table was an equally long row of windows that looked out into the forest next to the house. Unlike the living room, it was reasonably clean, which had my brain asking all sorts of questions. Why would someone keep his kitchen tidy and leave the living room a mess?

I deposited the dishes in the dishwasher, then returned to the living room to wipe down the table. Miraculously, it seemed to have survived the abuse unscathed. I studied the mess, looking for more clues about this mystery family. The trucks and the dinosaur suggested the girl wasn't an all-pink type, and the lack of coasters on an expensive-looking table suggested a comfort with their wealth. Old money. Though kids' toys and the lack of adult items indicated Sofia was the center of this household, the abandonment of this room cast a sadness over her absence. When had Edward and

Rebecca split? If it was recent, the living arrangements would be new for Sofia.

Since this room was dominated by Sofia's things, I decided to make it into a sort of welcome home for her. The room's state made me think it wouldn't be used until she was back anyways. I piled the books and miscellaneous toys onto the coffee table. Starting with the largest stuffed bear, I chose a tutu from the dress-up clothes pile and fitted it over the bear's lumpy waist. I sat it in the center of the sofa, then worked my way through the rest of the stuffies, finding hats and capes for them. I arranged the animals along the sofa, interspersed with plastic dinosaurs and a robot-looking thing so they were all seated in a long row, with two fluffy little owls sitting on the largest bear's lap. Next, I tackled the books, propping them on the stuffies' laps and in their paws. The octopus could hold four books at a time, and one of the larger bears held a book open for a dinosaur, as if it were conducting story hour.

I worked on this toy tableau, changing up combinations, making sure the books were the right size for each animal. Some of the smaller plastic dinosaurs were difficult to balance among the fluff, so I opened a book flat and arranged them in a semicircle around the picture, as if they were reading together. After I'd found a place for all the items, I leaned back on my heels, admiring my work. When Daisy was younger, she and I did this with her toys, and I wondered if Sofia would want to do this kind of thing too.

What was Sofia like?

I didn't hear the floors creak, but when I looked up, Edward was standing in the doorway. He had taken a shower, and his dark hair was combed off his face, accenting his angular jaw and piercing eyes. He looked more polished than he had before. More distant.

"How long have you been standing there?"

He shrugged, like the answer didn't matter, and I guess it didn't, considering this was his place. A flush crept up my neck as I imagined him standing and watching me work. No, I definitely should not turn this into something sexual. Especially since I was now a sweaty mess. I smoothed the halo of curls that was springing out from my ponytail and stood.

"Have you decided on my fate?" I'd meant it to sound like a joke, but it came out more desperate than anything else.

Edward was frowning again. "It's not a good idea for you to stay."

The words came out firm and definite, settling with a heaviness on me. I looked at the ground, fighting the urge to cry. I knew this job was too good to be true, something out of a book, not the life that I was living. Just as I'd finally escaped my family, I was being sent back to them. Back to my sister, who would no doubt try to get me to do something for her, and back to my mother, who needed me to share her load. As much as I wanted to help, I also wanted just one summer to myself. But this guy wasn't responsible for helping me escape my dysfunctional family. I was coming back in a week…hopefully.

I stood and forced myself to meet his gaze. "I understand."

But Edward wasn't looking at me. He was gazing at the couch. He crossed the room and came over next to me, inspecting my work. I looked too, trying to focus on my creation and not the freshly showered, very male scent of him, nor the news he'd just delivered. It was the first time I'd been this close, and I was getting a clear reminder of why staying alone with this man really wasn't a good idea for me.

Edward stared at the different groups of animals, and after a while, he turned to me. Close up, his eyes were impossible to ignore. So dark, so serious. I swallowed.

"Could you do this in Sofia's room?"

I was so stunned at the question and focused on the letdown that I just blinked at him.

"I'm sure her room is a mess," he continued. "If she came back and found her room like this, it would… It would be good."

"Yes, of course," I said, my tongue tripping over my words. I had impressed him, and the thrill of pleasing him was making my brain spin. I drew in a quick breath, waiting for what came next.

He seemed to be studying me. I fought the urge to look away and kept my gaze steady on him. I fought not to get distracted by the fullness of his lips.

"I prefer to be left alone during the days," he said.

"Yes, of course."

"No one will be available to attend to you."

Attend to me? What *was* this place? I bit my lip to hold back my smile. "That's not a problem."

He continued to look at me, and heat crept up my neck and pooled further down between my legs.

"Then I suppose you can stay."

"Thank you," I whispered. "You won't regret this."

He looked back down at the sofa with an expression that said, *I probably will.*

But he could think whatever he wanted. I wasn't going to be sent back to the US. My new, improvised job wasn't clear, but as long as it didn't involve living with my family, I was pretty much okay with anything.

"I'll show you to your room," he said and started toward the front hall. I followed him. He headed across the wooden floor, toward the staircase, and I took a quick detour to grab my suitcase.

Clop. Clop. I followed him up, my suitcase banging on each step.

I made it two steps before Edward stopped and turned around, frowning at me again. My face burned as I squirmed under his displeasure and my fine-tuned attentiveness to it.

"Sorry," I said quickly. "I'll carry it."

"I'll get your suitcase," he said, then added gruffly, "I should have thought of that."

"Thank you." I wondered how often he actually had to carry anything up the steps. If "the staff" was here, this would be someone else's job. But I was grateful. Edward lifted my suitcase with surprising ease and carried it up the stairs in front of me. He was tall and lean and… I forced myself to look away.

At the top of the stairs, Edward paused on the landing, next to the balcony railing.

"This is the east wing," he said, gesturing to my left. "Your suite is on this end, as is Sofia's bedroom."

I looked down the hallway and nodded. It was brighter than the downstairs halls, with light coming in through the long, slim windows at both ends. The rain beat against them, loud and insistent. The ceilings were tall and airy, lined with the same plaster moldings and flourishes I had seen downstairs. Old Romantic-era landscape paintings hung on the walls, filled with tempestuous skies and moody fields.

"My rooms are in the west wing, in case of an emergency." He gestured in the other direction, then repeated, "*Emergency.*"

I nodded, trying hard not to imagine his bedroom.

"These are the stairs to the attic. It is off-limits." His voice had an ominous tone to it. He pointed to a door opposite the staircase, with the same type of brass handle and skeleton key slot I'd seen downstairs.

"I understand," I said softly, my gaze lingering on the door.

"Good."

He started down the hallway, still pulling my suitcase, and I followed him.

"This is a guestroom, and that is Sofia's bedroom." We passed the two doors he pointed at, then came to a stop at the end of the hall. "This is Sofia's playroom, and you will be staying in the suite across the hall."

He gestured toward a door opposite Sofia's. My heart sped up as we walked to the door, and I told myself not to get my hopes up, no matter how promising the word "suite" sounded. Despite my attempts at pessimism, my heart thumped faster. Not just a room. *My own suite.* I didn't care what it looked like as long as it was mine.

Edward turned the old brass handle, and the door swung open. He gestured for me to enter. I took a few slow steps as the room came into view. The dark sky cast a muted light on the white walls. There was a desk and a bed, and an old-fashioned lounge chair in red velvet, but all I could see was the view. The side of the house looked out over the gazebo and pine forest, a mix of bright and dark greens, the distant treetops disappearing in the mist. That would have been more than enough, but the back view was even more breathtaking. Between tall pairs of windows was a set of French doors that led out to a balcony. My very own balcony. I had slowed in the middle of the room, and now I started for the doors. I peered out into the misty rain falling on the back lawn. What I couldn't see from the first-floor living room now came into view: just down a gentle slope, the Baltic Sea churned, the wind whipping up whitecaps. I swallowed back a surge of excitement. This was so much better, so much more than I had hoped for.

I don't know how long I stood there, greedily taking in everything I could see, but when I turned around, Edward was still standing at the doorway.

"Thank you for letting me stay," I said, emotion spilling into my voice. "This is incredible."

He tilted his head a little, like he was actually looking at me.

"When she gets older, this will be Sofia's room," he said quietly. "But she is still too young to trust with her own balcony."

"Lucky me," I whispered to myself.

I suppressed a yawn. Now that the uncertainty of my arrival was passing, the jet lag was hitting me. I'd been awake for… How many hours? Too many. And right now, it was catching up with me.

"Do you need to sleep?" he asked.

"I think so."

I was also hungry, but the thought of crossing the house and finding my way back to the kitchen sounded too exhausting to undertake.

"I'll leave you to settle in." After a pause, he added, "We can talk about your job in more detail tomorrow morning."

Edward walked out and closed the door, and I was left alone in the most luxurious room I had ever stayed in. My eyelids were heavy, and I told myself I could explore tomorrow. Right now, I needed sleep. I opened one of the packs of cookies I'd stowed away from the plane ride, hoping it would get me through the night. Then I fished my toothbrush and toothpaste out of my handbag and stumbled into the bathroom, too tired to admire the old basin sink and footed bathtub. Instead, I brushed my teeth, then headed straight for the bed, pulled aside the fluffy covers, and climbed in, fully dressed.

I had no idea what the next week would bring, but right now, I could sleep in this quiet room and be utterly alone. I could do anything I wanted without worrying about who else might come in or need my help.

I closed my eyes, letting the exhaustion take over. But as I drifted off to sleep, it occurred to me that I still didn't have a charger for my phone.

*

I awoke to the patter of rain on the windows, a little disoriented and a lot hungry. I opened my eyes, and the room came into focus. The red velvet chair, the French doors onto the balcony… I was in a *foreign country*, sleeping in my *very own bedroom suite*. I let out a long sigh and tried to sit up, but my dress was tangled in the covers. Right…I hadn't changed last night, and now my dress was digging into my waist. I hadn't slept this well in years. What time was it?

I looked out the window at the tips of the pine trees in the grey mist. The sky was about the same as it had been when I fell asleep, though Sweden was known for its midnight sun. I looked around the room for a clock but found nothing.

Regardless of the time, I was hungry and more than a little uncomfortable. Aside from the cookies, the last time I'd eaten was on the plane. I rubbed my eyes and gazed across the room at the gilded oval mirror across from the bed. My hair was a tousled mess, and my dress looked…well, like I'd just slept in it. I wasn't going to make the best second impression like this, and considering the precariousness of my situation, I figured it counted.

I rolled out of bed and dug through my handbag for a couple more packs of cookies, downing them hungrily, then headed to my bathroom to inspect this newfound luxury. It had been renovated, judging from the gleaming white tiles and polished silver fixtures—either that or the place was kept in top shape by "the staff." The latter seemed more probable. I opened the narrow linen closet and found a stack of fluffy white towels. I grabbed two and hung them on the empty rack. After years of wet towel coordination with my family, this was another luxury. The floor was warm under my feet, which meant…floor heating? It was almost too good to be true.

A few minutes later, I stood under a cascade of blissfully warm water. I washed my hair and then just closed my eyes, though I was unable to stop bracing myself for my sister to barge in and tell me to stop fogging up the bathroom because she needed to put on her makeup.

My hair was on the long side, and I had a whole curl-taming strategy that involved products and a blow dryer, but I was far too hungry to bother with that, so I simply ran a brush through it a few times and toweled it off the best I could. I headed back for my suitcase and pulled out my white button-up and a grey pinstriped skirt, a little wrinkly but basically fine. I slipped on pearl earrings and sandals, then glanced in the mirror again. Much better. My cheeks, pink from the shower, and my wet hair both made me look younger, but hopefully my outfit balanced out the look.

My stomach growled again. I opened the door and peeked into the hallway. Was Edward awake? I waited a minute, but I heard nothing, so I crept into the hall and made my way to the kitchen, marveling once again at the stillness of this place. It was hard to imagine that people lived like this all the time.

I entered the kitchen, a little overwhelmed by the sheer size of it. There was what looked like a fresh loaf of French bread on the counter, along with a small basket of assorted fruits, neither of which I had seen when I was cleaning. I reached for an apple but hesitated. I was a stranger in this house. Was I allowed to eat whatever I wanted, or did Edward have official mealtimes? Four-course meals were the kind of thing I'd expect from a house like this, but I couldn't ask. And it felt strange to make myself at home anywhere, let alone in an old-fashioned manor house. Then again, Edward said not to disturb him. I didn't have much choice but to take him at his word.

I gingerly tugged open the fridge and found it full. I spent some time trying to decipher what everything was. The words "milk" and "yogurt" looked similar enough to English, and packages of cheese and ham and grapes were recognizable. There were also plenty of homemade meals in glass containers, all labeled in indecipherable words. Safe breakfast foods or unrecognizable dinners? The clock on the stove read 7:38, though I wasn't sure if that meant morning or evening.

Just as I reached for what looked like a tomato-y kind of stew, the floor creaked behind me. I looked over my shoulder and found Edward in the doorway. He had caught me standing with his refrigerator door open, a cardinal sin in my household. I quickly closed it and straightened.

Edward was freshly showered again, his dark hair glistening and wet, making the blue in his eyes stand out. He was dressed in new clothes, a button-down shirt and grey slacks this time, which made me think that it was 7:38 a.m. Which meant I had slept through the entire night. No wonder I was so hungry. I also noted our outfits matched. I had no idea what people wore in extravagant manor houses like this, but at least for the moment, I was appropriately dressed.

"Um, hi," I said, trying not to get flustered. "I was just getting something to eat."

"Of course." He seemed to use this phrase to convey many different things. In this case, I was pretty sure it meant "this was obvious," which I guess it was.

"I'm sorry," I said automatically, then mentally kicked myself. What was I sorry for?

He ignored my apology. "After you eat, I'll give you a tour of the grounds, and we can discuss what I need from you, both this week and when Sofia arrives."

I smiled. "That would be great."

He didn't smile back. "I'll be in the library, just off the front hall."

Without another word, he walked away, leaving me in a puddle of hot, unprofessional desire. What was *wrong* with me?

I gulped down some mysterious but tasty food, then headed for the library. I slowed as the hallway floor creaked under my sandals, thinking about facing Edward again. It was my chance to demonstrate that he had not, in fact, made a mistake by letting me stay.

I took a deep breath, then started toward the doorway on the other side of the hallway. As I approached, I spied wooden bookshelves with elaborate carvings lining the walls. A real library. I was spending the summer in a house with a library.

I walked forward, letting the scent of old books pull me in. There was a pair of tall windows on one side of the room and a stone fireplace on the other.

Everything else was books. I gazed at them, turning in a circle until Edward's profile came into sight. He was sitting in one of two tall-backed leather chairs, both angled around the fireplace. On a table next to him was a small pile of books and a reading lamp.

"I trust you found a suitable meal," he said, his eyebrows slightly raised.

I nodded, not sure if that was a real inquiry or a subtle critique for serving myself. I decided I'd be on better footing if I changed the subject.

"I've never been in a home library like this."

"It's my favorite room," said Edward, and I thought I caught a hint of wistfulness in his voice. "I used to hide in here from my nanny and try to read these books. I had no idea what they were about."

It was impossible to imagine him as a young boy, smaller, more vulnerable. As an adult, his voice was lush and rich with a little grit. It was perfectly tuned to the room, like he was a part of it.

"This job will likely be demanding," he continued. "My daughter has always been a bit headstrong, but since my wife and I split, that characteristic has become more prominent. Practically Perfect Nannies indicated that you could handle this."

"I can." This was pretty much the only part of this arrangement I was fully confident about.

"She is also very good at getting her way. We spent the first four years of her life in New York, with only the summers in Sweden. For those years, she was bilingual. However, since we returned to Sweden full-time, she has refused to speak English. Your main goal this summer is to make her speak again."

"I see." I was going to do my best, though making six-year-olds do things they didn't want to do wasn't usually the best way to establish a relationship with the kid. Still, I'd taken this job, so I'd figure that out.

"Let me know what kind of educational materials you need, and I'll get them."

I blinked. Did he think some sort of quasi-school situation was going to make his daughter more likely to speak? Hmm…

"Do you have children's books in English?" I asked.

"We should."

He didn't know? Now I was even more curious about their relationship. Was he just as formal with her as he was with me?

I trained my expression to neutral and said, "Can we look?"

He raised his eyebrows, as if he didn't expect to participate in this part of my job. But then he nodded.

Edward rose from his chair, and I headed into the hallway and up the stairs, trying not to think about the way the air seemed to crackle and sizzle when he was behind me. The best thing to do was ignore it.

He caught up at the top of the stairs and walked next to me, toward the door he'd indicated as Sofia's bedroom. The closer we came to her bedroom, the more

I sensed a tension from him. It wasn't that dark, broody cloud I'd felt when he told me the attic was off-limits. This was...something else. He stopped at her bedroom door. His chest rose and fell, and then he opened it.

Based on the state of the living room, I was perfectly ready for a mess of toys, but in front of me was the opposite. The room was sparsely decorated, with a four-poster bed as a centerpiece. It was draped with gauzy white material tied to the posts in each corner, forming a canopy. The bed was a heap of pillows and blankets, with a white duvet underneath and a few stuffed animals scattered on it. A few more had spilled onto the floor, the only evidence that an actual child lived here. In the corner was a matching armchair, its pillows fluffed and untouched. There were no bookshelves, and the bedside table held just a clock and a lamp. Nothing whimsical, nothing personal, aside from the stuffed animals. It looked like what an adult thought a kid's bedroom should look like.

I wandered in, trying to mesh this room with the mess I'd found in the living room. I peeked into a walk-in closet full of color-coded clothing and neatly arranged shoes. Still no books or toys. It was the most bizarre room I'd ever seen for a six-year-old kid, like something out of a Victorian-era childrearing textbook. I struggled to figure out how to convey worries in a way that wouldn't get me fired. But Edward spoke first.

"Sofia sleeps in the smaller room since she's too young for her own bathroom at this point."

I nodded, keeping my expression neutral. Did he think I was quietly contemplating the injustice of his daughter's living arrangements?

"She doesn't appear to have any books," I said carefully.

"They're probably in her playroom." He frowned a little, and, in that moment, I realized what that tension I'd seen outside the bedroom door was. Uncertainty.

I closed the closet doors, and we left, Edward leading the way. When he opened the playroom door, the mess I'd expected in the bedroom appeared. Legos, dress-up clothes, and puzzle pieces were scattered around, along with a new population of stuffed animals, which seemed to multiply by themselves in this household. Plus, there were books. Some were on the bookshelves, but others lay on the ground, in the hammock-like seat that hung from the ceiling, and inside a little tent in the corner. So this was the room she actually used. And good news: She seemed to be a reader.

"There must be something here in English," said Edward with an offhand wave of his hand. I was getting a pretty good picture of how much time he spent in his daughter's rooms.

I gave him a professional smile. "I'll work on organizing and see what you have, and then I can find an English-language bookstore in Stockholm to fill in the gaps."

"I'll have them delivered." He gave a curt shake of his head as if to end the discussion, and I followed him back down the hall.

"The rest of the upstairs is mostly bedrooms," he said, gesturing first to the bedroom next to mine, then down the hall to the west wing. There were four or five of them, and I tried to imagine the house bustling with guests. It felt like something that might have happened long ago, far in the past.

As we passed the door to the attic, a cool shiver ran through me. I glanced at Edward. That gloomy pall had descended over his striking features again. My mind went straight to Jane Eyre and Mr. Rochester's secret wife he locked in the attic. *Rein in your imagination, Ava.* Any curiosity about what was behind those doors needed to be tempered with my interest in keeping my job.

Edward led us down the stairs and into a more formal living room, filled with stuffy furniture, the kind that looked like no one had sat in it for the last hundred years. I followed him, tripping over a rug and then bumping into an end table. I couldn't help but be transfixed by all this luxury.

"Sofia will generally be here Monday through Friday and away for the weekends, with a few exceptions," he said, leading us back into the dark hallway. "Your day will begin at 8:00 a.m. and end at 6:00 p.m., with a break every afternoon when Sofia and I take the boat out. You are responsible for preparing breakfast for Sofia, and Britt-Marie, the cook, arrives at 11:00 a.m. to prepare lunch and supper."

Did he eat meals with his daughter? It wasn't the kind of thing I should ask, though I suspected I knew the answer.

We passed a den of sorts, dark and mysterious. I made a note to explore that room later.

"That's my study," said Edward, gesturing to a door on one side of the hallway, then turned to a door on the other side. "And that's Rebecca's."

I waited for him to explain the present tense he'd used, but he seemed to be done with that subject. We exited onto a terrace through the French doors in the main living room, just across from the toy tableau I'd organized. The rain had mostly let up, and the air was heavy and damp. Tangles of rambling roses climbed up the columns and twisted around the beams, filling the space with their heady scent. The forest wasn't far, lurking on both sides in the mist, and in front of us was the sloping, green hillside. There was a stone pathway that led toward the water, and I could make out the Baltic in the distance.

Edward grabbed an umbrella leaning by the door. He opened it and headed for the stone path, then looked over his shoulder, like he was waiting for me to join him. We walked side by side down the path, his elbow brushing against my arm, each touch making me aware of just how close he was.

"This is the gardening shed," he said, tilting his chin toward a building that was probably the size of my family's apartment. "It used to serve as the pantry years ago, but we've managed to move that indoors."

Was that a hint of dry humor? I glanced up at him, but I couldn't tell from his expression.

"The forest trails make for good walks so long as you are careful not to get lost," he continued, nodding in the direction where the path branched off, toward the pine trees. "We've gotten plenty of rain this year, so the blueberries should be ripening."

I tried to imagine this buttoned-up man picking blueberries in the woods…and failed. We continued across the lawn until the shore came into view. Down a meandering stone stairway was a private sand beach in a little cove, surrounded by a shoreline of large, flat stones. Next to the beach was a building, somewhere between a cabin and a barn, and farther around the cove was a wooden dock with a flashy-looking speedboat and an old, wooden sailboat, the rich, brown wood carefully preserved.

"That place is off-limits," he said, gesturing toward the building.

I nodded dutifully.

"The nanny agency assured us that you would have lifeguarding certifications," he said, looking at the stormy sea.

"I do."

"Sofia loves to swim, but she is not to go anywhere near the water unless she has a lifejacket on." The statement came out in that final, commanding tone.

These pronouncements sounded a little extreme, but then again, compared to the stories my mother had told me, this was far from the most eccentric wealthy family she'd run across, so I just smiled and said, "I'll make sure she does."

He turned back toward the house. I took one more glance at the seaside building, then followed. We walked back in silence, and he seemed lost in thought. When we stepped back onto the terrace, he turned, looking down at me, his brow furrowed. He parted his lips. Hesitated. Then spoke.

"I'm aware I'm not an easy man, but there is nothing I want more than my daughter's happiness."

I nodded.

"I want…" He looked unsure. "I would like you to help me figure out how to make her happy this summer."

The words were heavy, filled with that uncertainty that seemed to come out every time the subject of Sofia came up.

"I'll do my very best," I said softly.

He held my gaze for an extra beat, then gave one of his curt nods and disappeared into the house. I don't know how long I stood there after he left, half-drunk on the scent of roses and Edward.

Chapter 3

At first, I was perfectly content to spend the rest of my day alone. This house was the opposite of an apartment, where you were in everybody's business whether or not you wanted to be. Here, I was blissfully free to sleep or eat or wander around the house and its grounds whenever I wanted. It was freeing. And then I remembered my phone.

I'd left a potentially worrisome message on the nanny agency's line yesterday that I should probably address, but I had forgotten to ask Edward about the phone charger. Where was he now? I took a couple tentative steps into the house and stopped, listening for signs of movement. Nothing.

I ran upstairs and grabbed my phone, then sank onto my bed as I waited for it to turn on. The bright screen flashed, as did the red low-battery bar. Six percent. I didn't bother reading any of my messages, just typed a quick one to the agency:

The client is allowing me to stay at their home until the official start date. Everything is resolved.

I let my family and Ruthie know I'd arrived safely, then powered off the phone again. After setting it on my bedside table, I listened for the creak of Edward's footsteps. They didn't come, so I went downstairs, peeking into the living rooms and the studies, but the downstairs was still and silent too. I gave up and decided to focus on my first task: organizing Sofia's room.

It only took a few minutes to learn that Edward was right. His daughter did have a few books in English, though they looked untouched on her bookshelves, unlike the others that were scattered everywhere. I spent a few hours in her room, slowly organizing and taking stock of what toys she seemed to prefer. Unlike her bedroom, decorated in princess-y themes and colors, she seemed to prefer dinosaurs, stuffed animals, and green-themed puzzles. I quickly used my phone to search for a way to order more books, and after a few stumbles, I received a message that they'd arrive within a week.

When I was tired and hungry again, I headed for the kitchen for another exceptionally good meal, a sort of stroganoff, though I was pretty sure I'd never tasted this kind of meat before. The clock above the kitchen stove told me it was 5:00 p.m., but my body felt done for the day. I returned to my room and dug through my suitcase for a book, but by the time I changed into pajamas and climbed into bed, I was too tired to do anything but close my eyes.

My sleep was long and full of dreams of Edward and of this strange new place, so different than anywhere I'd ever been. My mind kept coming back to the door to the attic, the door Edward had explicitly forbidden me to enter. In daylight, I'd promised not to open it. In my dreams, I trespassed.

My mind went to places that I wouldn't allow it to go during the day. In one dream, I crept toward the attic door in the darkness. I rested my hand on the cool brass, and as I turned the knob, the storm clouds rumbled outside. Suddenly Edward was there, dark and moody, pressing me up against the wall with his hard body.

I warned you, he whispered.

Another dream was more explicit, with him naked over me, his muscles taut and his face unreadable as his hard length pressed against me.

I warned you.

But the most disturbing dream was the one where Edward didn't appear. The attic door was ajar, and just inside was an ancient stone staircase that spiraled into darkness. The stairs were cold and dank as I started up, knowing something was waiting at the top. Or someone. With every step, the fear gathered in my chest. Still, I continued, pulled by whatever was up there. Finally, when I rounded the last corner, just before the attic came in to view, I woke up.

I lay awake for a long time after that dream, my mind racing. The house was quiet, and I had the sense that it was the middle of the night, despite the grey twilight coming in from the windows. After some tossing and turning, I got out of bed and walked over to the French doors, opening them to the heavy summer breeze. I stepped onto the balcony and breathed in the salty sea air.

But what drew my attention was the light coming from the seaside building. What time was it? I crept into Sofia's room and checked the clock. 2:36 a.m. Was Edward down there in the middle of the night? If so, what was he doing? I lay back in my bed, trying to figure out the answer, but I came up with nothing.

The next day, just as I was waking, I heard the stairs creak. Edward was close, and I needed to talk to him about a phone charger. I jumped out of bed, grabbed my phone, and ran down the hall. When I reached the top of the stairs, he was almost out of sight.

"Mr. Vallenberg?" I called.

He froze, then slowly turned around, his expression blank. I raced down the wooden stairs, clinging to the banister.

"I'm sorry to disturb you, but I forgot my phone charger," I said breathlessly, the words tumbling out as I came to a stop in front of him. "I was wondering if you might be able to tell me where I could buy a new one? It's this kind."

I held out my phone, plug side out, as evidence. His Adam's apple bobbed as he swallowed, and the muscles of his jaw worked, tense and restrained. He was looking at me, not my phone. Suddenly, I was aware that I was in sleep shorts and a tank top with no bra. Awareness prickled through me, pooling between my legs. I looked down at my nipples, poking through the thin fabric of my top.

I peeked up at Edward again. His blank mask had cracked. His full lips were parted, and his eyes were dark and heavy with lust. Desire crackled through me, sharp and electric. My breath was an audible gasp. The moment the sound escaped from my mouth, his expression shuttered closed.

"I'll put an appropriate phone charger on the kitchen counter," he said in that formal way he had and disappeared down the hallway.

I spent the morning organizing Sofia's room, and by the time I went to the kitchen, there was an octopus-like cord on the countertop. One of the dangling arms fit my phone perfectly. I plugged it in and listened to my messages.

There was one from my mother, telling me she'd call me soon, and one from Practically Perfect Nannies, letting me know that Edward's assistant confirmed that I would, in fact, be paid for this extra week. The last message was from Ruthie. I left my mother a message, but Ruthie picked up on the first ring.

"How's your new, mysterious job?"

I filled her in on the house, the mix-up, and Edward's reluctant invitation to stay.

"If he sends you home, you know you can always crash on my floor."

"Thanks."

A burst of warmth flowed through me as the familiarity of her voice came through my phone. As happy as I was to have some space from my family this summer, I didn't want to be away from Ruthie.

"And Viking land? Have you met any hot, bearded men yet?"

"Umm…"

"Wait, let me guess," she deadpanned. "You're going to tell me that your boss is hot."

My face heated up as my mind went back to my more explicit dreams. "No comment. But that's not the biggest problem. Not only am I a week early, but Mr. Vallenberg is divorced, and the daughter isn't here yet."

Ruthie let out a loud laugh. "So you're living alone with your hot, rich boss for a week, the one you swore you would not fall for this time?"

I sighed. "Maybe? And I'm spending the week organizing his daughter's room."

"Oh, Ava." she sounded more serious now. "I don't have to remind you about what happened with Matteo."

"I know. It's not going to happen again," I said quickly, not feeling at all sure. While the Dr. Chu thing had remained one-sided, Matteo was another story.

Somehow I had found myself getting more and more flirtatious with him until he invited me to his place. I pointed out that I probably shouldn't since he was my boss, and I lost that job quickly afterward. "Seriously, I learned my lesson. It's not going to happen this time."

"Okay. Just remember that you can't trust a powerful man. They do things to get that power, things you don't want to know about."

My mind went straight to the attic in my dreams, so I told my mind to shut up. "He's old money."

"So his ancestors did the dirty work, and he just kept the family business running. Is that better?"

We were both silent as I contemplated that.

"Forget him," said Ruthie. "You need to get out there. Go out to some club this weekend and meet someone else. Those Vikings are all hot, right?"

I knew she was right, at least about the distracting myself, but leaving this place was the last thing I wanted to do. I'd waited my whole life for this kind of quiet, this kind of freedom. I'd just have to find a way to get Edward out of my mind.

"I'll think of something," I said.

There was a pause, and then Ruthie sighed. "I have to get ready for work, but let me know how it goes."

"I'll send you an update soon."

"You better."

*

I spent the mornings cleaning and organizing Sofia's room, learning everything I could about her from the toys that looked well loved. This left my afternoons for exploring the house. The library was my favorite room, of course. I sat in Edward's chair, gazing at the titles on the shelves, wondering which ones he'd read. They were all in Swedish, but I didn't care. Just the heavy scent of old books and the dark shelves surrounding me were enough.

But I grew restless. I'd been an apartment-dweller my whole life and was not used to spending so much time in one place. I ventured outside, wandering around the property. The clouds cast moody shadows on the forest, and the air was still and cool. I walked along the trails, careful to keep the house in sight. As I made my way around each new boulder, I half expected Edward to appear, his gaze piercing through me. It was easy to wander too far from the house, down sloping hills and along winding trails. I found a little stream, clear and cold on my fingers. I took off my shoes to feel the icy water rush around my feet, reveling in the sensation.

Days floated by, and suddenly, the week was over. Sofia was arriving the next day, and I only had found three English-language books to use to connect with her, all of which were about boats. Hopefully the new ones would be delivered before Sofia came. Of course, Edward was nowhere to be found. I hadn't seen him since that morning I'd rushed down the stairs, woefully underdressed, though there were times I could have sworn I'd felt him watching me. Or maybe this was my way of dreaming of a life that was never meant for me. Edward's life, here in this old manor house, definitely wasn't.

I searched for him all day, and by the time I lay in bed, I still hadn't found him. Storm clouds had turned to rain, pattering on the window. I dozed off, dreaming of secret forest paths and shadows, but I was awakened by a loud clap of thunder. It rattled the walls, and in the attic above me, there was a crash. I sat up, startled in the darkness. I reached for my lamp, but no matter how many times I flicked the switch, it didn't turn on. Above me, something rolled ominously. For the first time, my fascination with this house edged toward fear. I grabbed a long cardigan and ran to the doorway. No lights anywhere. I tried a switch in the hallway, but nothing happened.

"Mr. Vallenberg?" I called.

My voice echoed down the empty hallway. His bedroom was off-limits—implied if not stated, but I was past the point of caring. I wasn't even sure which room was his, but I ran down the hallway, past the attic door and into the west wing, knocking on doors as I passed them.

"Edward?" My voice trembled this time. "The lights went out and I need…"

What did I need? I told myself I just wanted some sort of grounding. I wanted to remind myself that ghosts weren't real, that this house wasn't haunted. I didn't let myself think any further than that. I came to the last door, panting. I knocked, but there was still no sign of life.

Maybe he was awake. Maybe somewhere downstairs. I headed down the staircase.

"Edward?" I called again into the darkness of the first floor.

The only sound came from the rumble of thunder and the creak of the staircase under me. I padded into the living room, the wood floor cool under my bare feet. Out the window, I spotted a dim glow of light. I couldn't see the shore from here, but the light was coming from the area of that seaside building. Was he there? Relief rushed through me at the possibility.

Before I could think better of it, I was out the door, heading toward the dim glow. The forest on both sides was enveloped in a cloud of ghostly mist, closing in on me. I ran across the flagstone trail, clutching my cardigan tightly as the drops of rain hit me. A flash of lightning lit the tempestuous sea in front of me. I started down the stone staircase as white-capped waves crashed against the rocks. The seaside building came into view, the taller part barely an outline. Only the front room was lit.

I ran across the sand and up the stairs, coming to a stop under the little porch roof. Up close, the building was older than I'd expected, with deep red paint covering the weathered wooden siding. Lights glowed from the scattered windows on the sides, but I couldn't see anything. The rain pelted the roof above me.

Now that I was here, I was no longer sure why I'd come. Fear had driven me out of my bedroom and out of the dark rattling of the house, but what was I looking for from Edward? He'd done his best to avoid me this week, so I knew better than to look for comfort. The best I could hope for was that electric connection I felt when he was near. Just the way he looked at me with authority and desire, held at bay behind that stuffy exterior—somehow, that might be enough.

I shivered, soaked through, as I raised my hand and knocked. The sound barely reached my ears over the wind and rain, so I knocked again, harder.

"Mr. Vallenberg?" My teeth chattered as I spoke. "Edward?"

Surely this counted as an exception to the rules. I contemplated baring the rain again to look through the front windows, but they were too high for me to see from the beach below. I banged against the door with my fist.

"Please."

Maybe he wasn't here? If not, then maybe he'd never know if I went in. I rested my hand on the knob and turned it. The door was unlocked. I took a deep breath and pulled it open.

Edward stood in front of me, and it wasn't the buttoned-up Edward that had taken me for a manor tour and told me the schedule in his precise British English. No, this was the Edward I'd caught a glimpse of that first day. His hair was a disheveled mess, as if he'd just woken up. One sleeve of his elegant shirt was rolled, and another dangled down, neglected. His expensive slacks were wrinkled, and he smelled of whiskey. I'd almost forgotten about the whiff of alcohol I'd caught that first day. His expression was dark, thunderous.

My body was coming to life as he glared at me, his entire being focused on me. *Oh*, this feeling. Ruthie would tell me that it was unhealthy, but I didn't care. What it felt like right now was pure bliss.

"This place is off-limits," he said, his voice thick and rough. "I made that clear."

He was going to turn me away. I could feel it, and it was worse than facing his haunted house alone.

"It's just that the power went out, and something crashed in the attic…"

My voice trailed off as his gaze dipped down to my lips.

"You're pale and shivering," he growled. His chest heaved as he took in my soaked cardigan and bare feet, then muttered something under his breath. We stood still, our gazes connected, as I waited for the second time for him to determine my fate.

"Come in," he finally said, stepping back.

I entered the little front room, distracted by the zip of electricity as my shoulder brushed against his chest. It was a small room, almost like an enclosed porch, with furniture that looked much newer than anything in the house. Edward grabbed a fleecy throw blanket from the sofa and handed it to me, and I wrapped it around my shoulders.

"You have no umbrella and are barely dressed, and you're running through the rain in the middle of the night—" With each word he spoke, he moved a little closer, and now he was standing so close that I could feel the heat from him, radiating, calling to me. He hung his head, his breaths on my neck, so deliciously warm and intimate. "Why are you here, Ava?"

It was the first time he'd spoken my name, I realized. The intimacy of hearing it that deep, raspy voice set off an entirely different kind of shiver inside.

Slowly, I lifted my gaze, taking in the heavy rise and fall of his chest, the sharp ticking of his pulse at the base of his neck, those beautiful soft lips, the hard planes of his cheekbones, until I finally met his eyes. They were dark, his lashes heavy, and it felt like he was going to devour me. And, *oh*, I wanted to beg him for it.

"I told you to stay away," he said. It sounded like half a warning, half a plea.

My mind was taking this to another level, going to places I knew I shouldn't go. But still, I let my next thought slip out of my mouth.

"Then I guess you should punish me."

He stilled. I had taken this too far. I froze as his hard stare settled on me, volatile, explosive. I had just ruined everything. But then a deep groan escaped him, and before I could take my next breath, his mouth came down on mine. The kiss was hard, rough, uncompromising. It was exactly what I had asked for, a punishment, so deliciously brutal that I moaned. His teeth scraped my lips, and I kissed him back, searching for more. Heat raced through me, pooling between my legs, pushing away the chill as his hands found my hips, my waist. I couldn't wait to see what further punishment lay in store for me.

I lost my balance and stepped back, and he followed me until my back was against the door. He rested one hand on the cool wood above me, the loose sleeve dangling, a reminder of his carefully kept façade of control that was coming apart.

"Is this what you came for?" he asked, his teeth gazing my neck.

"Yes," I whispered.

He pressed his hips against mine, his hard cock fitted perfectly against me. I reached for it, but he gave me a stern shake of his head. "Off-limits."

The words only made me want to defy him.

"I've tried so hard to resist. Just a taste." His voice was hoarse, and I wasn't sure he was even talking to me.

He opened my cardigan, exposing my tank top, soaked and sheer. He sucked in a breath and raised one hand to my breast, cupping it with his long, beautiful fingers. Then he bent down and took my nipple in his mouth. An electric jolt ran through me as he sucked on it through my shirt. I cried out, twisting his hair in my fingers, pulling him closer. His breath was a groan, and then he found my other breast, taking the nipple between his teeth this time.

The sheer bliss of his mouth overwhelmed me. Was this really happening? Maybe, before I completely lost my mind, I should tell him this would be my first… Except if I told him I was a virgin, I was pretty sure it would make him stop.

"This is wrong," he whispered, his mouth brushing against my sensitive skin.

Those words were a current of pleasure that shot through me, and all I wanted was more. His hand traveled lower over my shorts, brushing between my legs. I couldn't let this stop.

"Just a taste," he said again, more to himself than to me, it seemed.

He knelt in front of me, and my body went taut with anticipation. My hands trembled as I hooked my fingers under the waistband of my shorts, soaked through from the rain. I eased them over my hips, down my thighs, keeping my gaze fixed on the desire that was cracking through Edward's stoic expression. It was unspeakably arousing to watch his stern exterior crumble. I did the same for my panties, then dropped the blanket and my cardigan on the floor. Edward's jaw worked as he watched. Slowly, I lifted my tank top over my belly, over my breasts, over my head, leaving my hair to drip water down my body in trails. I was naked, and Edward was fully dressed and kneeling before me like a man at an altar. I ached for him to worship me.

But he didn't move. His gaze traveled up my body like a lick of pleasure, turning my insides molten. The throb of his pulse was the only other movement I saw. His hands were balled in fists, as if he were holding himself back, resisting. Even half-asleep and at the bottom of his whiskey bottle, Edward was fighting to keep himself in check, and the longer he did, the more anxious I was that he would put a stop to this. I itched to reach for him, for him to reach for me, but he just stared at me with those piercing eyes.

"Please," I whimpered.

"What are you begging for?"

Your body. Your cock. More. "You."

He shook his head, but his expression was pained, like it hurt him to refuse me. I sucked in a breath, trying to rein in my disappointment. He frowned. Swallowed. Let out a long breath.

"Just a taste," he said, his voice a raspy whisper.

Before I could respond, his hands were on my skin, touching me, caressing my hips, stroking my thighs, my belly, lighting new trails of heat. He brought his mouth closer until his lips brushed against me, and all rational thought left my mind. He eased my leg up over his shoulder until I was open for him.

His eyes fluttered closed as he inhaled, then groaned. A few, incomprehensible words fell from his mouth, whispered like a prayer, and then his lips found my clit. A kiss. A breath. His tongue. Slowly, devastatingly slowly, he began to devour me. My body trembled. I reached for him, needing something to hold, and he let out a low, guttural sound. His fingers caressed my rear, my thighs, and then they entered me, setting off new streaks of pleasure. I was panting and moaning and past the point of caring as he deliberately drove me crazy. It was too much and not enough, but he was relentless, building and building until my body exploded and I came. Lightning flashed through the windows as I cried out, my words lost in the thunder.

Seconds, maybe even minutes passed, and I realized that I was sitting on Edward's shoulder. My legs must have given out at some point, and my whole body felt blissfully lethargic. My hands were still tangled in his hair. I let go and tried to stand, but my legs were shaking under me.

"Let me help," said Edward.

His voice was controlled. I looked down and found him staring up at me, his expression somewhere between satisfaction and longing. He unhooked my knee but held onto my hips firmly, making sure I didn't crumble to the ground, waiting until I was no longer wobbly. When he was satisfied, he stood but didn't move to unzip his trousers, despite the thick erection that pressed against the expensive wool. In my experience, admittedly limited to movies, books, and my sister Brenda's stories, men didn't stop at this point. I watched his Adam's apple bob in a hard swallow. Edward closed his eyes and drew in a breath, and when he opened them again, I could see he was backing away. I reached for him. He caught my wrist and gently but firmly returned it to my side.

"But—"

He cut my words off with a shake of his head. After another heave of his chest, he reached for a new blanket and wrapped it around me. Then, before I could fully register what was happening, he picked me up in his arms and opened the door. He carried me out into the rain, up the stone steps, and across the path. Lightning lit the sky, and the manor house glowed in the mist, but in Edward's arms, my fears dimmed.

He headed into the house, walking through the living room and the hallway and up the stairs. He was now soaked too, and his wet lips were close enough to kiss. But I knew he didn't want that, so I rested my head against his chest, listening to the thump of his heartbeat. I was half-asleep as he laid me in my bed, naked but warm. He pulled up my covers and paused, his gaze traveling down my body one last time.

"This can never happen again," he said with a frown, then disappeared into the night.

Chapter 4

I awoke that night and couldn't fall asleep again, reliving the moments in that little room in the seaside cottage over and over as the lightning flashed and the thunder rattled the glass of my windows. This was no longer just another one of my crushes. I could still feel Edward's breaths on my neck. I could still hear the waiver in his voice as he said *off-limits*. Did he know these words added fuel to the fire that had started inside me a week ago, burning relentlessly, despite all my attempts to douse it? If those words were meant to quash my lust for him, he had failed miserably. He didn't know the way desire and longing lured me in and hold me under their spell.

I had never tried to fight my crushes, mostly because I never expected something to happen. And in the case of Matteo Romano, when the opportunity presented itself—or, rather, he presented himself to me—messing around with my much-older boss immediately lost its appeal. This time was so different. This time the hunger I saw in Edward made me burn brighter.

Was Edward thinking about me right now? Probably not. Off-limits for him meant…well, off-limits. He was an extraordinarily disciplined man, after all. As far as I could tell, he had gone for days without contact with anyone, except for a few shreds of interactions with me. I tried to picture him in his bedroom, at the other end of the hall, but the vulnerability of him lying undressed in his bed, drifting off to sleep was too much for my mind to process.

But there was something else blooming in me, something new. His touch, his need had shifted more than just the balance of our boss/employee relationship. It shifted something in me too. All these years I'd lived with fantasies in my head. I'd spent enough time distanced from my life, dreaming from afar of experiences I wanted. Walking into one of my fantasies didn't just mean experiencing them in three dimensions. It was messier, different. *I* felt different, though I didn't understand how.

I lay in bed, looking out the window at the Baltic Sea, lit by the glow of never-ending twilight, and listening to the storm, until I finally drifted off to sleep. My dreams were strange and dark, more feelings than scenes, and I woke up wondering if I had imagined the whole night at the seaside building. It was all so unbelievable that I might have doubted the whole experience if there weren't trails of whisker burns on my breasts, down my neck, between my legs.

I was groggy enough that it took me a moment to figure out what was different. There were sounds of movement in the house. Voices. I sat up in bed, disoriented, until I remembered. Today Sofia was coming, so "the staff" had returned. Which meant Edward and I were no longer alone in the house.

I scrambled out of bed and headed for the shower, letting the water warm my body. I was extraordinarily curious to meet Sofia and almost just as curious about Rebecca, whom I was hoping to get a glimpse of. I also wanted to meet the other staff, who were the closest I'd have to co-workers this summer. My family had always been the staff, and while I was thrilled with the idea that a household with a cook meant I'd get a break from cooking and cleaning this summer, I couldn't imagine being comfortable with that arrangement. My mother had come home talking about the eccentricities and dirty laundry of too many families to believe that I wouldn't be judged.

I showered and blew my hair dry, then put on a white dress with little blue dogs on it. It was wholesome and yet playful, which I hoped would strike the right tone with Sofia. I then headed out downstairs and into the kitchen. A woman about my mother's age was there, surrounded by bags of food that she was unpacking. She paused as I entered, her gaze traveling down me in one efficient sweep, then went back to unloading the bag in front of her. My face flushed at her cool dismissal.

"I'm Ava. The nanny." I bit my lip. She wasn't stupid. Of course I was the nanny.

"Britt-Marie." She paused and added something else in Swedish, though I wasn't sure it was for me.

I gave myself a mental kick. Maybe she didn't speak English. Of course everyone in this country hadn't mastered my own language the way Edward had. I had worried about this factor enough to consider not taking the job. But the last week of listening to the most delicious-sounding accent rolling off Edward's tongue had somehow made me forget about this issue.

"Breakfast?" I tried, then pointed to the spread on the table. She met my gaze for a moment, then went back to her work.

The table was covered with a spread of cold foods and an overflowing vase of flowers. There were cartons of yogurt and an assortment of cereals, as well as a basket of breads, a tub of butter, cheeses, cold cuts, sliced vegetables, and a fruit salad. I crossed the kitchen and sat tentatively at the table, unsure of whether I was even allowed to eat this food or if it was just for Edward. But Britt-Marie did nothing to stop me, so I peered into the basket, took out a slice of soft brown bread and buttered it. I took a bite, wondering if she was watching what I ate out of the corner of her eye. As I took my second bite, a piece of paper caught my eye. It was folded in half and propped against a lone coffee mug, and my name was printed in the front in blocky script. I grabbed it eagerly, a blush rising to my cheeks. I took a deep breath and opened it.

Sofia will arrive at 10:00 a.m. Please be in the front hallway by 9:45.

My heart sank. But what had I hoped for? A love note with hearts and flowers? I refolded the note and stuffed it in my pocket.

The books arrived at the front door as promised, and I occupied my time arranging them in the playroom. At 9:45 a.m., I stood in the front hall, clasping my hands behind my back like a good staff member. I still hadn't seen Edward. Not that that was unusual, but after last night, I had hoped to at least pass him in the hallway, just to understand if last night changed things for us. The last thing I had said to the man was about punishing me, which was so far out of line that my cheeks flamed just thinking about it. What had made me say that? But I know exactly what it was. I had wanted to push him, nudge him just a little more, and yet I ended up showing my whole hand. What had felt tempting last night now sounded incredibly brash in the light of day. I needed to somehow reassure him that it would absolutely not happen—

My heart jumped as footsteps came from the library. Then Edward was there, right in front of me. He didn't look at all surprised to see me, which meant he had likely heard me walk down the stairs. He had made me wait for him. The idea sent a strange and thrilling burst of heat through me, and I swallowed, trying to tamp down my reaction. I forced myself to think of other things. Like empty bank accounts. And moving back in with my family.

"Ava." My name came out precisely, crisp, in that glorious British accent. Maybe I could have resisted the accent alone, if it didn't come in that smoky bedroom voice of his. It was a combination of both that really did me in. It made each thing that came out of his mouth sound like a come-on. I knew it wasn't, but my body was trying to tell me otherwise.

"Mr. Vallenberg."

He frowned. "I apologize for my—"

"Please don't," I said, cutting him off.

I think my interruption surprised us both. He raised his eyebrows. I'd told myself that I should say the minimum, just go back to being the staff, quiet and obedient, but the words came out anyway.

"It's your right to regret last night, but it was everything I wanted. Please don't take that away from me." I kept my voice low, trying not to let it carry back to the kitchen or wherever else staff members were lurking.

Edward's brow creased, like he was weighing what I said. He took a step toward me, then another. Waves of heat crackled inside me, and the tension between us wound tighter and tighter. I wanted to say something, but the words were stuck in the back of my throat. His face was inscrutable as ever, but I could see the beat of his pulse at the base of his neck ticking, hard and insistent. His eyes rested on me, and my breath hitched as he took a step closer, then another. His hands clenched, then released. Those gloriously long fingers had caressed me, pleasured me, as they traveled over my skin. My breasts grew heavy, and I longed to feel those fingers on my skin again…

The crunch of gravel under tires broke the silence of the hallway. All the tension between us dissolved. I told myself that this was what should happen. Edward's daughter was here, and he was my boss, so measured, so aloof and in control. He was a man who would hold that line between us, and I should be grateful for that.

Except I wasn't. Warning bells went off in my head. *Be careful*. This was the kind of thinking that could cost an extra semester in tuition or a perfectly good job that promised me a way out of my family's apartment.

So I straightened up, took a deep breath, and watched as Edward used those beautiful fingers to open the door.

The scent of roses wafted into the house, and I took a long, dreamy breath as I stared at the black town car, parked at the end of the front path. The driver opened the rear door, and Rebecca stepped out. I stared at her through the doorway, mesmerized. She was even lovelier in real life than she was in the pictures. My first thought was relief: Edward didn't lock her up in the attic like we were all in some Gothic novel. Of course I didn't really believe that, but somehow my brain still hadn't let go of the idea. The second thing I noticed was a crackle of interest pooling in my body.

Rebecca was tall and slim, and she moved with an easy, graceful flow that made the simple act of stepping out of the car into a dance. I was captivated. Her blond hair was tied back neatly, and her dress was a pale blue, stylish and modern. She had a magnetic presence. I could feel it radiating down the walkway, into the house, under my skin. I looked down at the dog print on my sundress, shifting uncomfortably. Instead of playful and inviting, I looked childish. Edward and Rebecca were two forces of nature, and I was a leaf, swirling around at their whim. Rebecca was what this house was missing. She was what Edward was missing.

Then Sofia stepped out of the car, and I tore my eyes from Rebecca to watch her. The girl was a little copy of her mother, with poise and an understated yellow dress. Her hair was in a single long braid down her back, but it was the look on her face that I was drawn to. She had a serene, unflappable not-smile, as if she didn't notice the fact that she was being chauffeured. As if she didn't notice she was walking in to a home that was bigger than my entire apartment building. This should have come off as annoying, a six-year-old who was immune to her place at the top of the economic hierarchy, but it didn't. Instead, she looked innocent, like she didn't even understand her position. This was the girl Edward had described as headstrong?

Mother and daughter walked up the path like two, self-contained islands. I drew in a breath, my surprise giving way to nervousness. Since I had read about the bonus for staying longer, I'd been preparing myself for the kind of spoiled, bratty behavior endemic in the high-paying nanny jobs in New York. It's why I had taken this job, despite my complete lack of knowledge about Sweden or Swedish—because I could handle that. But everything about this girl in front of me seemed to present a completely different kind of challenge. She looked so self-contained, so impervious. I was starting to understand her resistance to speaking English a little better. This girl wouldn't be coaxed by standard methods.

Sofia walked inside the house first and headed straight for Edward. She looked up at him and said something in Swedish, and he picked her up into a tight hug. They stayed like that, her arms around his neck, her eyes closed, and what I felt first was a mix of warmth and relief. I have been wrong, at least a little bit. She wasn't completely impervious. Edward had spoken about his love for her, and I could feel the deep truth of that statement.

My gaze darted back to Rebecca. She had come through the doorway too, and she wasn't studying Edward and Sofia the way I was. She was looking at me, sizing me up. Strangely, my body lit up under her gaze. I could feel that this was a game. I didn't know what the rules were, but my body was begging to play anyway. It was as if last night had opened up a new, unruly want inside, and I didn't know what to do with it. She raised her eyebrows, then turned and said something to Edward.

He set Sofia on the floor and said, "Sofia, this is Ava. She came here from New York, and she will be your nanny this summer."

Sofia looked at me with her wide blue eyes and nodded.

Rebecca said something else in Swedish, and she turned to look at me again. Edward responded, his voice sharp, and she laughed. I was getting a very strong sense that this exchange was about me by their glances. I remembered the way his eyes had narrowed with anger and bitterness when he'd spoken the word *wife* that first day, and I saw a glimpse of it flashing in his eyes today. Through this exchange, Sofia just stared at me, almost as if she wasn't hearing her parents, like she was in her own world now. I shifted, feeling all of the discomfort Sofia didn't seem to register. Were these two going to argue in front of their daughter?

The same thing must have occurred to Edward because he glanced down at Sofia and frowned. Rebecca looked down too, and as if by tacit agreement, the tension between them ended. Rebecca was the one who broke the hard stillness echoing in the hallway. She bent to give Sofia a hug. For some reason, I'd expected her to be just as cool toward Sofia as she was toward Edward, but she wasn't. There was real love, real affection as she squeezed and rubbed noses with her daughter. I gave myself an internal kick at the assumptions I'd made. Sexy wasn't the opposite of a good mother. Rebecca said a few words, then turned and walked away, down the front path. Edward closed the door behind her, his expression stony.

I was pretty sure I was officially on duty now, so I took a deep breath and smiled at Sofia. "Shall we take your suitcase up to your room?"

She gave a little nod, so I grabbed the suitcase, and we started for the stairs. I could feel Edward's eyes on us, and I tried to push him and the whole scene that had unfolded out of my mind. I could mull over that later. Instead, I thought about what might be going through Sofia's head right now. I remembered a time before my father had left for good when my parents' arguments had gotten intense. The fights were about all sorts of things, maybe a splurge purchase by my mother or a stretch of nights at the bar by my father, but they almost always came back to money problems. It was impossible not to fight in front of the kids in a little apartment, so they didn't even make an effort. The fights left an indelible mark on me, an undertone of fear about the instability of our family. Sofia's life was so different than mine, and yet I had a strong sense that this piece wasn't so different. From a young age, I'd found my own escape in books. Did she find ways to escape too?

If Sofia were six-year-old me, I would have wanted to be alone in my room right now, losing myself in another world, in a story where I knew everything would turn out happily in the end. I didn't know what she wanted, but I was pretty sure that leaving her alone right now wouldn't be good first-day-on-the-job behavior. I had to come up with something else.

At the top of the stairs, Sofia silently took the handle from me and rolled her suitcase into her bedroom. I watched her lay it carefully in the corner next to her closet. She unzipped it and pulled out a raggedy, dark brown teddy bear. The bear got a quick hug, and then she placed it in the center of her bed, with the other animals. I was once again struck by the contrast of her two rooms, this tidy, staged room and the mess of her playroom. Right now, she seemed perfectly at home in this little palace, which made me even more curious about her.

"I have a surprise for you," I said. "In your playroom."

She nodded and came to join me. Edward had mentioned that her English understanding was good. Many parents tended to overestimate the brilliance of their children, but so far she seemed to be comfortable with my language. It also occurred to me that she was completely unfazed that I, a stranger, had appeared at her house, and she was expected to go with me. She probably had more experience with nannying than I did.

We walked down the hallway, our footsteps echoing in the now-quiet house. As I rested my hand on the door, I found I was nervous. I really wanted her to like my creation. The door swung open, and Sofia took a few steps, then came to a stop, gazing around her room. I held my breath, waiting.

I'd wanted to do something a little more personal with her playroom than I'd done downstairs. After all, this was her room, and I wanted her to feel free to play. My first idea had been a tea party, but what if she wasn't a tea party kind of child? But when the books arrived, the perfect idea came to me.

The books were my gift to her, so I'd wanted to make that sentiment at the center. I'd chosen a stuffed dinosaur, one that had enough wear to make me suspect it was an old favorite, and I created a birthday party for it. The books were the presents, of course, and I wrapped them in squares from the long roll of butcher paper on Sofia's easel, then used her markers to decorate them with animals. I'd positioned the tea set and the food toys to create a birthday picnic feast, and I'd gathered other stuffed animals as friends, one for each book. I dressed the smaller ones in doll clothes and the larger in kid-sized dress-up. The attendees all held the wrapped books, and a little white rabbit was handing one to the dinosaur.

I looked down at Sofia. She was staring at the tableau, her lips parted and her eyes wide.

"These books are yours to unwrap," I said. "I thought we could read them together."

She looked up at me, and the smile that lit her face made my breath catch in my throat. Whatever else happened in this mysterious house, I was determined to be the nanny Sofia needed this summer.

We didn't see Edward for the rest of the day. At lunch, Britt-Marie gave me a note from Edward telling us that sailing was canceled, so Sofia and I spent the afternoon in her room, reading and exploring. She unwrapped each book carefully, saving the paper I'd decorated, which I took as a good sign. She hadn't spoken at all, but she seemed to understand most of what I had said. It made me wonder how quiet she was in Swedish.

At six o'clock sharp, I delivered her to Britt-Marie, as instructed.

"Your supper is on the counter," she said, gesturing to a tray with dishes hidden under silver covers.

I was momentarily stunned at her English, which was more than serviceable. Language wasn't a barrier between us. Britt-Marie had simply chosen not to speak with me this morning. Once I registered that knowledge, the implication of her statement hit me. I was expected to eat somewhere other than the kitchen.

"Thank you," I choked out.

I waved to Sofia and grabbed my tray, though I had no idea where to go. But I wanted to walk away as quickly as I could, so I headed down the hall and up the stairs, straight for my room. At least this was my own space.

And I had a balcony.

I hadn't spent much time there because of the rain, but the view was beautiful, with the Baltic shimmering in the distance. I opened the French doors and stepped out into the cool air. I set my tray on the little wooden table in the corner and grabbed a towel from inside to wipe the last of the rain from my chair, then sank down into it. The forest trees rustled in the breeze off the sea as I lifted off a silver cover, revealing a plate of meatballs, potatoes and something lumpy and red on the side. Under another was a small salad with wedges of tomato and cucumber neatly arranged on it, and the third tiny silver cover was hiding three buttery-looking cookies. After an overwhelming day, I was hungry, really hungry. I ate a meatball whole while I searched my phone for Swedish meatball meals. Lingonberry—that's what the sauce was. I dipped my fork into it and tasted. It was like...Thanksgiving cranberry sauce. Interesting. I speared another meatball and dipped it into the lingonberries, the way the internet said I was supposed to eat it.

But before I could take a bite, I heard the sound of a voice, Britt-Marie's, I thought, then Edward's, followed by the clink of a glass. I stood up and peeked over my balcony, but there was no one else outside that I could see. The voices seemed to be coming through the windows, the ones propped open just below my room. These were the dining room windows, I realized. Sofia said something, and then I heard the scrape of silverware on a plate. I returned to my chair, feeling a bit like a voyeur, but it wasn't spying if I didn't understand the language, was it? I was reassured to hear they were eating dinner together. As I speared another meatball with my fork, I listened as their voices came through the window. At first a conversation seems stilted. Edward said something, and Sofia replied with just a word or two. Then something changed. After one of Edward's questions or comments, Sofia's words began to flow. Sentence after musical sentence, she went on in her quiet, lilting voice. The more I listened, the more I wondered about this strange and compelling family.

Chapter 5

I barely saw Edward at all, though he never to my knowledge left the property. We communicated through notes, or, rather, he communicated with me.

Sofia should not go near the water without a life jacket.

Make sure Sofia eats more than bread and butter for lunch.

Sofia will not be visiting her mother on the weekends.

I thought about this last note for a long time. It was probably for the best since it meant Edward and I would no longer be alone in the house.

The rain had cleared, but the air was cool. In the mornings, Sofia and I read and built small cities with her Legos. She mostly preferred her playroom, but occasionally we ventured down to the informal living room where I found her toys the first day. Edward passed through from time to time, and I could feel his eyes on us. This was natural, of course. Clients wanted to know what their nannies were up to with their most precious kids. So why did I feel like his eyes were burning through me? I tried to keep those thoughts at bay, but at night they came in full force. I lay awake, replaying that night in the boathouse. I thought about Rebecca, with her penetrating gaze. That thought brought on a strange mix of desire, jealousy and curiosity that made me twist and turn in my quiet bedroom.

Sofia still hadn't spoken a word to me, and I wasn't expecting it anytime soon. There were some kids who loved to talk, who thrived on connecting their experiences with those around them. Sofia was not one of these kids. She was like her father in this way, as far as I could tell. Parents usually hired a nanny for their kids because they needed looking after, but even at six, she seemed like she could take care of herself better than my older sister could. So far, she was the most tranquil six-year-old I had ever met, though she definitely had a mind of her own. I guess I could see what Edward meant when he called her headstrong, but I was more inclined to describe her as self-contained. Ostensibly, I was here to convince her to speak in English, but I also got the feeling that Edward was avoiding Sofia, staying just out of sight. But that couldn't be right.

She seemed to enjoy my company, as far as I could tell, so I tried not to worry about it. Every day after lunch, Sofia and I walked down to the beach, where

Edward waited for us. I'd only seen him in button-up shirts and expensive-looking slacks, so I'd had to hold back my surprise the first day I saw him on the beach in swim shorts and a T-shirt. I had tried hard not to think too much about his body, convincing myself he probably had a pampered, rich man's physique. It came as a shock that this was nowhere near the truth. Edward Vallenberg was inexplicably ripped, and it wasn't just the forearms I'd caught peeks of since the first day. Those lovely forearms led up to corded biceps that flexed every time he moved. Was the rest of the seaside building an enormous gym he kept all to himself? Maybe that was what he did all day—lifted weights. The image of him, alone, sweaty at a machine was both absurd and sexy enough that I had to bite my lip to avoid smiling. No, it must be something else.

On my hours off, I explored. Even on the sunniest of days, the house never lost its moody feel. It seemed as if the house was holding onto a deep sadness. It oozed from the walls and crept through the floorboards, pulling me in with its mysterious allure and yet pushing me away, a foreigner in every way.

I also did some snooping. I couldn't resist. Edward had declared the attic and his wing of the upstairs as off-limits, but he'd said nothing about the rest of the house. Not a word about the studies, for example. One day when Sofia and Edward were sailing and Britt-Marie was upstairs vacuuming, I stood between the two study doors, debating. I took a deep breath and opened the door to Rebecca's.

The inside had a sumptuous feel to it, all dark wood and reds. Rays of light peeked around the heavy red curtains and onto the Persian rug, and the baroque-style reading chair was upholstered in red, velvet-like fabric. The paintings in Rebecca's study were nothing like the bland landscapes that hung in the hallways. They overflowed with cherubs and mostly naked women and men, feeding each other grapes or just lounging in the decadence of the forest. If this were my study, I'd get nothing done. I'd just stare at the paintings all day.

The vacuum was still running upstairs, so I crossed the room and sat in the chair behind the desk. This one was leather, and it was cool under my legs. I found a stack of correspondences Rebecca had left behind. I sifted through it, understanding nothing—it was all in Swedish, of course. In the top drawer there was an open wooden box with dividers that held monogrammed stationery, *RV* in calligraphy at the top of each paper, and a few expensive-looking pens lay in another compartment. I touched the monogram, smooth against the heavy paper.

The second drawer had the same kind of wooden box inside, and this one was filled with what seem to be carefully curated memorabilia. There was Rebecca in a photograph at the top of the stack. Next to her was Edward, smiling up at me. The two of them were at some sort of black-tie event, and she'd turned for the camera in a careful, flattering pose. But as curious as I was about her, I couldn't help but stare at Edward. Seeing him in a tux had its own appeal, but what drew me in was his smile. It was a good-natured smile, unguarded. This was the polar opposite of the brooding man that walked these hallways. I searched through the pile of photos. There were surprisingly few pictures of their daughter, just one with Sofia on Edward's shoulders, and a second with her at the zoo, pointing at an otter. Most of the photos were similar to the first I'd seen, just the two of them, taken at some formal event, but as I dug farther down, I found one of Edward lounging on a beach somewhere tropical, shirtless, the planes of his muscles on display. It was more than just heat that this stripped-down view of him sparked inside me. Jealousy and longing twisted with my desire. He must have been happy with Rebecca, and now he clearly wasn't. Why had they split? I stared at this version of Edward for another moment, then forced myself to move on.

I put the photos back in the drawer, making sure they were in the same order as I had found them, and looked at the next section. It was filled with media clippings. The first was from a newspaper and featured a photo of them with a caption. I pulled it out and read their names and the charity function that they had sponsored. It took a moment to register that I was reading it in English, which meant it was from their lives back in the US. There were more on that theme, clippings from newspapers and glossy magazines. Some of Rebecca, some of the two of them, but none of just Edward.

I was definitely snooping in their lives, and guilt was beginning to overpower my curiosity, so I shoved them back in. The last drawer had papers in folders, neatly labeled with categories I didn't understand. As I slid the drawer closed, it occurred to me that the vacuuming had stopped. As I rushed out of the room, hoping I hadn't left anything out of place, I heard Britt-Marie's footsteps on the staircase. I took a deep breath and headed the opposite direction.

The end of the week gave us the first truly warm day since I'd arrived. In New York, hot summer days were suffocating and smelly. Everyone who could afford it escaped to beach houses on Long Island or somewhere across the Long Island Sound. The rest of us suffered through it. I'd always dreaded summer heat waves, but here in Sweden, it was a completely new experience. The warm wind blew in through my balcony doors while the house itself managed to stay refreshingly cool. Probably all the stone and marble everywhere.

After our usual morning, Sofia and I walked down the path toward the Vallenbergs' private beach, the cool sea glittering in front of us. We had both changed into bathing suits and cover-ups after lunch. While she was out on one of the boats with Edward, I figured I'd read on the beach for an hour or two and maybe even take a swim.

"Is your father teaching you to sail?" I asked.

Sofia nodded. I'd quickly adapted to asking yes/no questions with her.

"Are you enjoying it?"

She considered this question for a moment, then nodded again.

"Your father must like it too."

She laughed a little, which I didn't really understand.

We came to the end of the grassy slope, where the beach house came into sight, and started down the steps to the water. It was so lovely down there, so quiet and peaceful, and once again I wished I could live in a place like this, in a cabin by the sea.

"Can you believe I've never been on a boat before?" I said, making conversation the way I usually did. I couldn't expect her to speak if I didn't set a good example. "I'm not sure if you remember how big New York is, but it's probably like downtown Stockholm, but bigger. Where I lived wasn't actually that far from the water, but that river wasn't the kind you go sailing on. There are ferries and tourist boats, but I've never been on them."

She looked up at me, wide-eyed. I noticed that she seemed very curious when I talked about New York, and it made me wonder how much she remembered from when she lived there. The Vallenbergs had been Practically Perfect Nannies clients then too, and I assumed her former nanny took her around to parks and museums.

"I've dipped my toes in the Atlantic a couple times, at the beach near Coney Island," I continued. "I even went in all the way one time. Actually, my sister pushed me in, but then she and her boyfriend and my niece jumped in too. It was hot enough that it felt good."

The memory of that day was vivid and warm, and for the first time since I'd arrived, I realized I missed my family. Not quite enough to want to go back, at least not at this point, but I no longer wanted to escape the way I had before.

We continued down the steps, the beach sparkling in the sun. The deck in front of the seaside cabin turned into a boardwalk that led to the dock, with benches and a picnic table that were weathered from the sea air. I decided I'd use them this afternoon. This was probably the closest I'd ever get to living a life of luxury, and I wanted to indulge in it for a few hours.

As we came to the bottom of the steps, Edward walked out of the cabin and across the sand. He was barefoot, and I couldn't help but notice that his feet were long and sexy, just like his hands. There was something intimate about seeing him like this. He looked more relaxed, the closest he came to that picture I'd seen of him on the beach. Or at least he did until he looked at me. His eyes perused my body, hot and focused as he took in my unprofessional outfit. Then he frowned.

"You're not going swimming alone, are you?" It came out more like a statement than a question.

"I haven't decided. Maybe just a little wading if I get hot."

I wasn't sure why he was asking. After all, it was my time.

The frown lines deepened, and a quick glance at Sofia told me she hadn't missed his displeasure. We stood there for a moment in silence, as I waited for his next comment. But before he could say anything, Sofia said something in Swedish. It was a surprise for me to hear her voice. After so many days of silence, I had almost forgotten that she did speak—just not to me.

Edward's eyes darted to her, and when she finished, he looked at me.

"You've never been on a boat?"

I blinked, as discomfort turned to embarrassment. I hadn't really meant that information for Edward. It only made me out to be that poor, unworldly girl he had hired, and while that dynamic was at the heart of my favorite Gothic novels, in reality, I didn't want to be anyone's charity case. In reality, I wanted him to respect me and see my skills for what they were…at least during the day. At night was another story. On the positive side, I had further confirmation that Sofia was keeping up with all my ramblings.

"Boats just haven't come up in my life, I suppose," I said crisply, though this was just a nicer way to say the same thing. Boats hadn't come up, in the same way as plane rides and tropical vacations hadn't come up either. It all boiled down to the same thing: we didn't have enough money to even bring these kinds of things up.

"You should come today. With us." It was a statement, made in a commanding tone, and I must have frowned because he added, "We'd like to invite you."

I searched for a way out of this as a wave of nervousness rippled through me. I wasn't sure it was wise to spend the day on a boat with the man from whom I was fighting to keep a professional distance, but when I glanced down at Sofia, she was looking up at me, and her face had lit up. I really couldn't say no.

"Okay, I'll go." I looked at Sofia and added, "Thank you."

"It's settled," he said in a way that sounded as much for himself as for the rest of us. Then he turned back in toward the deck, and Sofia followed him.

I passed the door I had entered that one fateful night, which I was trying very hard not to think about, and we continued to the other side of the building, to what looked like an upscale shed. He opened the barn-like doors to reveal water toys, rafts, paddles and lifejackets, all hung neatly, like they were waiting for a large family gathering. The beach and the main house were also like that, when I considered further, except there was no large family. It was just Edward and Sofia. For the first time, I felt sorry for them. What did it feel like to be here, just the two of them?

Ruthie's voice came next, laughing at my sympathy for a rich, white dude. She'd no doubt argue that the problem wasn't the lack of family. The problem was having too much for just two people. Still, it all felt a little sad.

Edward handed Sofia a life jacket. She snapped it on and ran for the dock. His back was to me as he rummaged through the collections until he chose one off the hook. "Check to see if this fits."

Of course, I'd never tried a life jacket on, so I fumbled a little, trying to fit the clasps over my chest. When I looked up, he was right in front of me. The electric sparks crackled and sizzled between us, and the pulse at the base of his neck ticked out those tempting beats, calling me. I tried to ignore them, but his eyes were heavy with desire. All the distance between us this last week fell away as he reached for the strap and said in that low, commanding voice of his, "Loosen the straps. Like this."

His hand brushed against mine, and I had to hold in my gasp. His jaw clenched, and I watched his Adam's apple bob as he swallowed.

He snapped the clasp of my lifejacket, and then he turned away. I let out a shaky breath. How was I going to survive on a boat with him for the next few hours?

I walked out of the shed toward the dock. Sofia had stopped along the way to nose through the picnic basket Britt-Marie had packed for the excursion.

"Finding anything good?" I asked.

She nodded and held up a glass jar full of cookies. Edward came out of the shed, and Sofia quickly closed up the basket again. I picked it up, and we headed toward the dock. The two boats were tied there with thick ropes, the motorboat, large and white with a cabin in front to protect from the elements, and the antique-looking sailboat, carefully constructed with row after row of wooden planks layered on top of each other. The sailboat was in beautiful condition—of course it was—like it had been lovingly varnished recently. I wondered what staff member was in charge of this meticulous job.

"I think we will take her on the sailboat," he said, glancing down at Sofia. "What do you think?"

She nodded and said something Swedish. It was interesting, the more I thought about it, how reluctant she was to speak in English. She wasn't exuberant, but she wasn't quiet, either. The more I thought about it, the more I wondered if this was her way of asserting herself.

Edward gestured to a set of wooden chairs. "Sofia and I will rig the sails. It won't take long."

I wandered down the dock, looking into the murky green waters and the reflections of the grey clouds moving above. I tried to imagine what it would be like to grow up like this, with the water so close. I found one of the well-worn chairs and watched as Edward and Sofia worked as a team, threading ropes through different pulleys, tying knots and pulling in the bumper buoys tied to the side. They worked with a quiet comfort of two people having done this countless times. I couldn't take my eyes off Edward. Every time he stretched up to grab hold of the sail or another rope, his shirt slid up, revealing a trail of dark hair that disappeared into his shorts. Every time he tightened a knot, his biceps flexed.

At last the boat was ready. Edward reached out his hand to help me in, and my breath caught in my throat. The flames I thought I'd stamped out sparked back to life. But Sofia was watching this time, so I fought to block out these feelings and reached for him. His warm hand enveloped mine, and for a moment I forgot to breathe. I quickly looked up, and his gaze met mine. I thought I caught a flicker of heat before his implacable expression was back.

Flustered, I stepped in…too quickly, as it turned out, because the whole boat rocked and swayed. Sofia let out a little squeak and grabbed the side of the boat, and Edward's other hand wrapped around my arm, steadying me. My breath stuttered, partly from the surprise, and partly because we were now face-to-face. Edward's eyes were dark.

"Don't make me regret bringing you," he murmured.

"Sorry," I said quickly.

I could have sworn the corners of his mouth twitched up.

After going over a few basic safety rules—rules that probably should have been covered before I stepped on, like stay seated and don't make any sudden moves in a small craft—Edward started the small motor on the back of the sailboat. Sofia untied the last rope holding us to the dock, and we started out toward the sea.

"Isn't a motor on a sailboat cheating?" I asked.

"This isn't a competition, Ava." Edward gave me a hint of a smile, and my heart thumped harder. "Sailing is whatever the wind wants it to be. And right now, in order to sail, we have to find that wind."

"Good point," I said, but what I was really thinking about was that smile. Since we had stepped onto the dock, there had been a shift. I hadn't noticed it at first, but the smile was too much to ignore. He just seemed more…*himself*, though I didn't know him well enough to say that.

Edward explain the basics of sailing to me, about something called tacking and switching sides when we turned—slowly, without fully standing up, he emphasized—and about making sure I didn't hit my head on the boom, the long pole that held the bottom of the sail. As soon as we were out of the little cove that protected his private beach, Edward cut the motor and tipped it up. Sofia took the steering stick at the back of the boat, whatever that was called. I was a little surprised he had just given the job over to a six-year-old, so I said, "Can I help?"

Sofia giggled, and Edward said dryly, "You can, by just staying where you are."

Then he started to raise the sails. It was mesmerizing to watch his muscles flex as he reached up, pulling the rope, then wrapping it around a series of mechanisms to secure it. He moved with a confidence, a sureness about him, which shouldn't have been a surprise, but I was impressed with his physical capability. His athletic build and sun-kissed skin were starting to make more sense now. I didn't know where to look. His calves were dusted with hair, his thighs corded with muscles, and the trail of hair down his abs… Now I was thinking about that trail. Which I absolutely shouldn't be. But before I could tear my eyes away, Edward caught me staring. His eyes widened, and I turned away quickly, looking out at the sea as my cheeks flushed with embarrassment.

As soon as the sails were fully raised, the boat took off. My embarrassment faded as the boat skimmed over the water, cutting through the waves, the spray coming off the sides. It was exhilarating as we picked up speed, just the sound of the wind and the splash of the water against the wooden sides. To think that for my whole life, I had never once been curious about what sailing might be like.

The roofs and spires of Stockholm poked through the trees, off in the distance, but we headed the other direction, into the Baltic. The sea was dotted with islands of flat rock, with patches of trees huddling in the centers. Some were larger, some tiny. Little red cabins and docks with flagpoles peeked out of some, and others looked untouched, with nothing but grey rock and pines. But the best part of the view was that it felt like we were alone. I thought back to New York, with its bustling streets. I thought about the subway and the crowds. Stockholm was probably like that, too. The land was ruled by people, but out here at sea, we were at the mercy of the wind and the rest of the elements. We were free.

It would have been enough just to sail, but as we came closer to a larger island, I could see that Edward had a destination in mind. Off one side of the shore were rows of docks, filled with speed boats and sailboats. As we drew closer, Edward pulled down the sail, and we motored over to a free spot. Sofia showed me how to put out bumpers to protect the boat.

At the end of the dock was an open space, almost like a park with a shed or a shelter of some kind, surrounded by a few picnic tables. It wasn't at all the kind of place I had expected Edward to frequent, but then again, none of this had been what I had expected.

"What is this place?"

"It's how I convinced Sofia to start sailing with me, right?" Edward patted his daughter on her knee, and she gave him a toothy grin and nodded. He passed her a wad of money, and she hopped out of the boat. I, on the other hand, slowly slid my butt onto the edge of the dock before I dared to stand up.

Edward said something to Sofia, and she took off. Then it was just the two of us. Edward wandered to the end of the dock, slipped off his shoes, and sat down, and I followed him. We were facing the sun, our feet dangling in the water. I realized that for the first time since I'd arrived, I wasn't nervous around him.

"I can't stand the suspense," I said. "What's going on?"

"This is her favorite ice cream stand," he said, and his smile was unmistakable this time.

I found that I was smiling too.

"I apologize for pressuring you to come with us," said Edward after a while.

I shook my head. "I loved everything about sailing."

Edward looked at me as if he was just as enchanted as I was. I wasn't sure if he was thinking about something more than the sailing, but I was.

Chapter 6

Somehow, I knew Edward would be down in the seaside cabin that evening. I had no idea why I knew, considering how mysterious I found so much about him, but I was sure of it.

I sat in the red chair in my room after supper, debating what to do with that knowledge. It was the kind of thing I'd usually talk to Ruthie about, hoping she'd give me a push one way or another, but I resisted calling her. Somehow, it just felt too private to share. The sea and the sun and Sofia had peeled back some of Edward's protective layers. I had gotten a glimpse of the man I'd seen in the photos Rebecca kept. I thought about the extensive NDA and the isolation of this house, lost in the forest. I thought about the initial distance I had felt between him and Sofia back in the house. I was missing pieces of this puzzle.

I wanted to go down to the cabin and look for those pieces. Would he be drinking by himself again? Would he have already retreated, gone back into that distant, closed version of himself? I couldn't deny the other hope that had swirled inside me since the last time I'd gone down to the shore at night. Was there a chance he would kiss me again…or more? My first experience with sex had left me craving, and the more I thought about Edward, using his well-muscled body all day long, the more my rational thoughts fluttered away.

I had spent my life holding back, letting wants turn to fantasies. This new summer version of me didn't have to sit on my balcony, wondering.

I look through my closet a few times, pulling out one flirty sundress, then another. Finally, I chose shorts and a tank top. Casual seemed like the right tone. The evening was still warm, and the breeze off the Baltic was refreshing. I passed Sofia's room, listening to Britt-Marie's voice through the door, then made my way down the stairs and out the French doors in the back of the house. The evening was bright, the endless summer sun still high, though more clouds had rolled in, casting shadows everywhere. I started down the path, breathing in the scent of the water. But the closer I came to the shore, the more uncertain I grew. Maybe I had just been a voyeur this afternoon, looking in on the intimacy of his relationship with Sofia. Maybe today wasn't about Edward and me at all.

I slowed to a stop on the steps, ready to turn back, when I caught sight of Edward on one of the deck chairs, looking up at me. He was wearing swim shorts and no shirt, and my stomach did funny things. But if I turned back now, I'd feel even more foolish.

I continued down, slowly, mentally kicking myself for not planning in advance what I was going to say. At the bottom of the stairs, I kicked off my sandals, hoping the sand under my feet would relax me a little.

As I approached the deck, I tried to keep my gaze off Edward's body and on his face. He was wearing his usual, inscrutable expression. I looked around for a bottle or a glass of whiskey, but I didn't see one. His hair was wet, as if he'd been swimming recently, which I found a little strange considering how he'd reacted when I'd contemplated swimming alone.

My heart kicked up higher as I climbed the two stairs to the deck.

"I thought there was a rule about no swimming without a lifejacket or two adults around," I said.

That comment earned a little smile, like he was well aware of this double standard, but he said nothing. It made me wonder how he could be so careful about everyone else's life but not his own. I stood in front of him, like a staff member waiting for instructions, and attraction flared up in me. Edward gestured to the chair nearest him, and I was relieved for the excuse to look away.

"You're good for Sofia," he said after a while.

"Even though she doesn't speak to me?" I smiled a little, like it was just a joke, but I had to admit I was nervous about this part. My job was to get her to speak, and I hadn't made any progress in that area.

"It usually takes a long time for her to warm up to anyone."

As far as praise went, this was lukewarm, and yet I could feel those familiar tendrils of desire curling through my body. I wanted so badly to please him, and any hint that I had was turning each tendril into something hotter.

I was searching for something to get my brain on another track when he turned to me, and for the first time that evening, it felt as if he was really looking at me. He watched me for a lingering moment. "Question for a question?"

"Definitely." I had so many questions.

He was silent for a while, and then he asked, "That first day, when you said you didn't want to go back. Why?"

I bit my lip. I didn't know how much I wanted to get into my family situation. Our lives were so different that it would be hard for him to understand. Then again, maybe it was better this way, to remind myself about how bad of a fit we were the moment we stepped back into his extravagant manor house.

"In our family, we need to work together to keep our apartment. And that means I take on a lot of things that need to be done. This summer gives me some breathing room while I'm helping to pay the debts we owe, but I knew if I went back, something would come up. I knew I wouldn't end up coming back to Sweden, and I didn't want that to happen."

I was afraid to look at him. I was sure I would find pity, and that was the last thing I wanted. But he said nothing, and the moment dragged out until I couldn't stand it any longer. I looked up at him, and he was wearing an expression I didn't understand.

"Your family takes care of each other."

"It's more out of necessity than anything else." But as the words left my mouth, I knew it wasn't the whole truth. Though after my father left, we didn't have much choice but to all pitch in, love was a factor too. It was the reason my mother worked two jobs, and it was the reason I'd picked up Daisy from school for years. "There's been a lot of hardship, but I love my family."

He seemed to accept this, so it was my turn to ask. The first thing that came to mind was a question I'd been wondering since Sofia arrived.

"Why don't you put Sofia to bed at night?"

I regretted the question immediately. I hadn't realized it could sound like an accusation, and I hadn't meant it that way at all. I was genuinely curious. Edward seemed to crave time with his daughter, and yet he left the most intimate parts of her day to someone else. He didn't say anything, just looked at me, until my face felt like it was about to burst into flames.

"You don't have to answer that," I said quietly. "I didn't mean to pry."

He looked out at the water, the sun flickering off the waves. "There are things that are hard for me to do. Normal family things that everyone else seems to do so effortlessly."

My breath caught at the pain the revelation revealed. "Like being in her playroom?"

He nodded. I'd suspected that the moment we'd walked in that first day and I'd seen his bewildered expression.

"But not sailing?"

He smiled a little. "Not sailing."

"And not meals together?"

"Supper is difficult, but I force myself to do it anyway."

These were ordinary, everyday things, but they were also the times that a parent and child grew closer. I'd done so many of these things for Daisy when no one else was around.

"But you watch us read," I added, referring to his habit of lingering in doorways and nearby hallways.

He chuckled. "Am I that obvious?"

"You're not the first parent to check up on their nanny. But usually it's to make sure I'm doing my job well."

"I can put myself through that pain, but I don't want to spread my..." He glanced at me. "...my struggles to her. It's better than her thinking she's the cause of my discomfort. She's young enough to think that."

The heaviness of his words hit me hard. I understood his logic, though I wasn't sure if that's what quiet, perceptive Sofia would think. But this was clearly something he spent years considering. Alarm bells were going off in my head. His brooding was about more than Rebecca. I was sure of it.

For some reason I thought again about those boring landscapes on the walls of the house in the places where I'd expected portraits. I'd expected it to be filled with shrines to Edward's ancestors, and yet this house had nothing that connected him to his family. I'd never even seen a photograph. It felt as though he'd given me a few more pieces of the puzzle, but I didn't know where they fit.

I didn't know anything about his past—the language barrier had stopped me from easy research. Could that be one of the reasons he had hired an American for the summer? Maybe I wasn't brought all the way from New York just because I would speak English to Sofia. Maybe having someone from far away was a little respite from whatever cloud was hanging over him. I knew the feeling of being exposed. When my father left, just walking down the street could feel like everyone was prying in on our grief.

"I'm so sorry," I whispered. "I really shouldn't have asked about that."

He blew out a breath. “It’s been a while since I’ve been around someone who doesn’t know my past.”

“We can keep it that way,” I said quickly.

“Ask me something else.”

I wanted to know so many things about him, about Rebecca, but I didn’t want to push him. I looked around, at the water and the beach and the forest that surrounded us.

“What’s in the rest of that building?” I pointed to the seaside cabin, the taller part without windows.

He looked a little surprised, and then he smiled. “I’ll show you.”

He stood up, and I looked away so that I didn’t watch the way his muscles moved again. It was hard to ignore his shirtless chest, the way he was so on display, so sexual. Edward tilted his chin in the direction of the cabin, and I followed him.

My heart raced as I walked, the sand clinging to my feet. I followed Edward up the steps and through the cabin door, into the little room. The place was less daunting in the daylight, without thunder shuddering around me. There were no bottles on the table in front of the sofa, and the small, antique-like table and chairs by the front window looked almost sweet. Still, the same mix of curiosity and arousal from that night echoed through me as we walked across the room.

Edward rested his hand on the handle, but he didn’t open the door. Instead, he turned to me. “What do you think is inside?”

I wanted to lie, but secrets and lies pulled people away from each other. I wanted to be closer to him. Still… "It's embarrassing."

He raised his eyebrows, waiting.

"When I first got here, I imagined myself living in the world of a Jane Eyre plot, so I had…ideas."

His eyebrows shot up in surprise. "Isn't that the book where the man keeps his wife locked in the attic?"

I flushed. It sounded much sillier aloud than it did in my head. "I mean, I wouldn't call it a fully formed theory. And I knew it wasn't true. It was just…"

He closed his eyes and swiped a hand over his face, and I could see I should have kept my mouth closed. But then he revealed a smile. His shoulders shook and…Edward was *laughing*. Embarrassment warred with the joy of seeing him so amused, so unfiltered. I bit my lip but couldn't stop myself from smiling.

"You have quite an imagination, Ava," he said as he turned the knob.

The door swung open, and I stepped into a cavernous room with a cement floor lit by high windows and light fixtures that hung from the ceiling. I breathed in the bite of fresh wood mixed with varnish. There was wood everywhere, long planks and a spread of power tools I couldn't identify. In the middle of the room was a skeleton of a boat. It was large, maybe twice as large as the sailboat we had been on, but the shape was the same. This definitely wasn't an attic prison for his wife.

"You're building a boat?"

Edward shook his head. "I'm restoring it."

I'd had the passing thought that he must have staff to keep up his other antique boat. I guess I was wrong. "By yourself?"

"This one is too big. There are parts I need some help with. But I did the one we sailed by myself."

I walked forward, looking at the carefully arranged pieces, bent and carved to make the frame of the boat. I ran my fingers over the smooth wood. It looked like the skeleton of a fish, with its fine bones rising up, a rib cage around the spine.

"It's beautiful," I said. "I can't believe that you can do this."

"I'll try not to take that personally," he said with a hint of amusement.

I flushed and opened my mouth to protest, to say that it wasn't personal, but my earlier thought that the staff had done the hard work suggested the opposite. It *was* personal. I had assumed that, because he was wealthy, he'd hire out any task that he didn't want to do. In fact, wasn't that what I thought about rich people hiring nannies? They handed off the hard tasks in life because they could afford to, and I realized I looked down on that.

But this project in front of me took so much labor, so much meticulous, hard work, and I found myself admiring it all the more because he didn't hire someone to do the difficult parts. Edward was willing to spend hours here, though he got help when he knew the job was too big for him. I wondered if he had hired a nanny for the same reason.

Edward was trailing behind me, and I could feel his eyes on me. I stopped by a workbench. There were various items scattered across it, a box of screws, a drill, and a pair of gloves, worn and molded in the shape of hands. Edward's hands. I brushed my fingers over one of them before I could think better of it.

"I never imagined all this."

"Instead, your first guess was that I was keeping Rebecca locked up here?" He leaned his hip against the workbench and crossed his arms. He was smiling, and though his words were filled with humor, I could see this was a challenge.

I bit my lip. "It made more sense in my head."

He was close, close enough that I could reach out and trace the muscles of his chest, his biceps, muscles that would flex as he hammered and sawed. I couldn't. I shouldn't. *Off-limits*. I swallowed, trying to look anywhere else.

But the electric current sparked to life between us, and a rush of desire surged deep inside me. Edward didn't move away. He took a step toward to me, his eyes dark, and somehow I found my back to the workbench. I was trying hard not to think about the memory of his hands on me, his mouth on me. I wanted to touch him so badly, and I balled my fist, determined to resist. Edward tilted his head down, his lips closer. His eyes were hooded.

"Off-limits," he whispered.

I wasn't sure if this was a warning or a come-on. Maybe it was both.

"Off-limits," I repeated, my voice was breathless and so full of the longing I was desperately trying to hold back.

"I told myself last time happened because I was drunk. That I gave in in a moment of weakness. But that was a lie." His mouth brushed the rim of my ear, sending a shiver of pleasure through me. "I'm losing my mind right now, trying to stop myself from having you right here, right in the middle of all this."

The words made my insides molten. "Do it."

He groaned, and then his mouth was on mine. My body rioted with lust and hunger, and his callused hands were rough, but his kiss was a caress, like he was savoring me. His tongue slipped between my lips, exploring, and I opened my mouth with a sigh. *Yes*. The kiss was sensual and slow, triggering something deeper than lust. It was as if every gasp, every brush against his skin, every connection I had felt these last weeks was distilled into this one, achingly slow kiss. Emotions were clattering against each other, loneliness, want, need, and others I didn't recognize. All the parts of me that I tried so hard to bury inside were bubbling up, and for the first time, I didn't want to bury them. I wanted to feel.

So I touched him. I pressed my hands against the muscles of his chest, and he made a deep, guttural sound that called to me. I threaded my hands in his hair and kissed him, pouring all my emotions into him. The shadow of scruff on his jaw scraped against me, teasing me, as I grew hungrier. I moved my hands down again, his muscles tightening under my fingertips, feeling the body I had watched all day. I explored, tracing the ridges along his stomach, luxuriating in each groan he gave. He let out another slow rumble as his tongue caressed mine in lush strokes. It was heaven. His kisses grew hungrier, and his hand slid down to my waist, over my hips, cupping my rear. He pulled me up against his hard length, pressed between my legs. We both groaned.

"You make me feel alive again," he whispered.

His words echoed deep inside me like a bell. *Alive.* I was alive with him, too. That's what this was. I wanted to tell him, but words were escaping me as sensations took over. All I could say was, "Yes."

His thick cock surged between my legs, and his eyes grew darker.

"I want you, Ava. And I swore I wouldn't do this."

Then, suddenly, he was gone. The heat, the delicious warmth of his body, it was gone. My breath caught in my throat at the hollow, aching need I felt. I needed more. I forced my hands to my sides, trying to catch my breath. His chest heaved, and Edward—aloof, controlled Edward—seemed to be struggling to get himself under control just as much as I was.

I don't know how long we stood there like that, just the sound of our breaths echoing in the workshop, as the events of the day clattered through my mind. He leaned forward and tucked a strand of my hair behind my ear, and there was so much tenderness in his touch that I thought maybe we could discuss this. Instead, he looked away. It was a dismissal, a polite one, but he got his message across.

Disappointment flooded through me. I tried to tell myself that he was right, but I didn't want him to be. My body ached for him.

I really should have left things the way they were. As a good employee, I would leave him alone, walk away, the way he wanted me to. But I couldn't. Or maybe I wouldn't. He had stopped the kiss from going further, and I would respect this, but the intimacy of these last moments emboldened me. Was it just the forbidden element of our encounters that made him back away, or was he also resisting the intimacy we were stumbling into? As I tamed the flames inside, more and more of the conversation from out on the deck echoed in my mind.

I was making connections I couldn't ignore: hiring a nanny and asking for help and the love he so clearly felt for Sofia but held back for some reason. I couldn't forget that first day, the vulnerability in his voice when he said he wanted to make his daughter happy. That first day he was asking for help, and even if I would never be anything but a nanny to him, I wanted to give him this help. I knew the ways sadness had pulled my own family apart, and if I could possibly help bring Edward and Sofia closer, I needed to try.

"Edward?"

He stopped, but he didn't turn around. "Yes?"

"What if you sat with Sofia while I read to her?"

I couldn't tell if he was surprised at my sudden change of topic. He said nothing. His shoulders rose and fell, and I could feel how much he wanted to walk away. It was the way he dealt with his struggles. His drinking, his self-isolation—these were all part of the same urge to escape. I was way out of my depth, far beyond what a nanny should concern herself with, and I knew any mention of this would bring up his guard again. I didn't want him to go back to the cool distance he had kept from me. But before long, I would be gone, and he and Sofia would still be here. Alone, together.

So I pushed him a little further, "You don't have to read, and if she sat on your lap, she wouldn't see your expression. We could try it."

Silence. My heart thumped in my chest as I waited.

"I'll do it any way you want. Whatever makes it work," I added.

I half expected him to tell me this was none of my business, and I would have welcomed it. Anything was better than this silence.

His shoulders rose and fell again, and he blew out a breath. Finally, he spoke.

"I'll think about it."

Chapter 7

I tossed and turned through the night. I dreamed of Edward, of my back against the workbench, of the feeling of his cock between my legs. But my mind didn't stop there. When the night was at its darkest, I dreamed of cries of pleasure coming from far away. I crept out of my room and down the hallway, the moody landscape paintings suggesting a storm brewing. I passed the staircase and continued into the forbidden wing of the house, following the grunts and moans. I knew where they were coming from. I stopped before Edward's door, breathless with curiosity and desire. I turned the knob and walked in. Edward was lying naked in the middle of the bed, tangled in red silk sheets, and Rebecca sat astride him, naked, her breasts bouncing as she slid up and down his cock.

She gave me a wicked smile. "You can join too."

My gaze darted to Edward. He just stared at me with dark, haunted eyes. I woke up before I had a chance to decide. The dreams felt real, solid, and in the space between waking and sleep, I couldn't sort out fantasy from reality. Or maybe I didn't want to. In the privacy of my room, I gave into the need that had built inside, pleasuring myself.

Days passed with Sofia, filled with puzzles and card games and treasure maps that took us through the house and across the grounds. Britt-Marie still hadn't warmed to me, and all my attempts to win her over fell very, very flat. I wanted to ask Edward about it, but I'd seen very little of him since that night in his workshop. There were times when I felt his presence, like he was just around the corner, but if he was there, he never revealed himself. The ache to return to the workshop came back at night, but even if he was there, I knew he'd turn me away. Instead, I was left with glimpses of him and the low melody of his voice through the dining-room window each evening as he and Sofia ate their supper.

After shaking off the last of my dreams one morning, I took Sofia down for breakfast, searching my mind for something new to explore. The day was warm, so I coaxed her outdoors on a walk to show me more of the paths through the forest. I followed Sofia, her lavender rain boots leaving thick prints in the soft earth. It had rained on and off during the night, and the forest floor was a rich brown. The scent of fallen leaves hung heavy in the mist. I was dressed in billowy trousers, a cream button-up shirt and a yellow cardigan, with a pair of sneakers that had never left the cement before I arrived here in Sweden. A wind blew off the sea, its cool tendrils weaving through the trees and underneath my sweater. Sofia led me down one path, then another and another until I was lost.

"You know where you're going, right?" I asked.

She smiled over her shoulder and nodded. The trail wove around boulders as we disappeared farther into the forest, farther than I had ever been. After climbing for a bit, the landscape flattened. We entered in a quiet grove of tall pines and the floor below was covered with short shrubs. The sun poked through the canopy, its rays filtering through the green. Sofia stooped down and peeked under the leaves of a plant. Before I understood what was happening, she popped something in her mouth. I froze.

"What did you just eat?" I asked, forcing myself to keep calm as I tried to recall my first aid class. Calling poison control was the first thing that came to mind, except we were in another country, where I couldn't speak the language. Should I call the one in the US? Now I was starting to panic.

Sofia bent down and came back up with a little, round, blue thing the size of a small pea, cupped in the palm of her hand. She held it out for me and smiled, but as soon as she saw my expression, her smile faded.

"Can you figure out a way to tell me what that is?" I asked, the panic leaking into my voice.

She tilted her head to the side, like she couldn't understand why I was so worried.

"I don't know what that is, but eating plants in the middle of the forest seems dangerous." My breaths were coming faster as my fear spiraled out of control.

"Blueberry." Her voice was soft, hesitant, and her cheeks flushed.

Relief came first, so it took a moment to register that she had spoken. *Sofia had spoken to me.* I was staring at her, so I looked down at her hand, trying not to make a bigger deal of this. Also, I needed to make sure she wasn't mistaken.

"Can I try?" I asked.

She nodded.

I bit into it, and the bright, crisp flavor filled my mouth. It was smaller than any blueberry I had ever seen, but the flavor was much stronger. It was, in fact, a blueberry, by far the best one I had tasted. The New Yorker in me still couldn't quite believe this was safe. I had never once eaten fruit straight from a plant before, and it seemed strange that we could just walk out into the forest and eat…for free. In a city, everything cost something.

I also couldn't get over the fact that Sofia had spoken to me. Could I get her to speak again?

"Is this your family's property?" I asked.

She shook her head.

"But we're allowed to eat these?"

"There is enough for everyone." Sofia gestured out into the forest, and I saw the same little plants spread out everywhere.

My heart took off. She'd spoken again. I noted that, unlike her father, she had an American accent.

Slowly, we continued down the trail, picking berries and eating them, and all the while I thought of Edward. I had to tell him. My heart leapt at the thrill that I had a reason to talk to him today, a reason to seek him out.

I waited until the evening, after dinner, and Britt-Marie was putting her to bed. I wanted to tell him alone, out of earshot from Sofia, but I was hoping to catch him in the house. I wasn't sure how I would react if I was alone in that enormous workshop with him. I glanced in the mirror and smoothed the curls that escaped my ponytail.

I walked down the steps and started through the quiet house, searching for Edward. The clouds cast shadows that danced across the walls as I made my way down the staircase. Sometimes it felt as if this old relic of a house came alive in the evenings, as if the walls themselves were watching me. I peeked into the library, then walked through the formal living room and the kitchen. As I wandered down the hallway, I saw the door to Edward's study was ajar. I pushed it open tentatively. Sunlight streamed through the tall, narrow windows, tinting the wooden bookshelves golden brown. I glanced first at the leather armchair, but it was empty. Edward sat behind the enormous wooden desk. His hair was neatly combed, and he wore a dark blue shirt, rolled at the sleeves. I forced myself not to stare at his forearms, at his long, capable fingers.

A messy pile of papers were stacked on one side of a large, leather blotter, and on the other side was a neat stack of envelopes. But he wasn't looking at the papers. He was looking at me. His eyes were stormy, both forbidding me to enter and luring me in. A few weeks ago, I would have backed away. Tonight I didn't. Instead, I stepped inside and closed the door behind me.

"I hope I'm not disturbing you, Mr. Vallenberg."

"*Edward.* Please, Ava."

"Edward," I repeated. The name felt intimate on my lips. His gaze felt intimate. Everything about this moment felt intimate, despite the fact that I stood across the room from him. My heart jumped in my chest, and my whole body was restless. I forced myself to stand still.

"I have news. Something happened today." I bit my lip, knowing how awkward I sounded.

He raised his eyebrows, waiting.

"Sofia spoke."

His eyebrows shot up, and all the cool distance in his gaze disappeared. I saw glimmers of happiness, the kind of uncomplicated happiness that was so unexpected from him, and I couldn't ignore how good it felt to please him.

He pushed back his chair and stood, then started around the desk toward me. My heart gave a hard thump, and I told myself he wasn't coming close for *that* reason. But my body didn't care. If his gaze felt intimate before, the way he was looking at me now was devastating. He stopped in front of me, so close I could touch him. If I dared.

"Tell me about it," he said. "Tell me everything."

So I told him about the walk through the forest and the clearing and the way she'd popped the blueberry into her mouth before I understood what was happening.

"I should get the number for poison control," I added.

He nodded, but amusement twinkled in his eyes.

"I'm from Brooklyn," I said a little defensively. "We don't have blueberry bushes growing out of the sidewalk in my neighborhood."

"I see."

I showed him my fingers, stained with the purple juices of excess. He took my hand as I spoke, caressing the stains, sending sparks through my body, and I wondered if he was trying to get closer to the experience. Or maybe this was something else. I tried to keep talking, but at some point my voice trailed off. The air between us seemed to crackle with electric heat. I watched, mesmerized, as he touched my fingers, my palms. Was he aware of the way this simple touch made my blood sing?

"I dreamed of you," I whispered, before I could think better of it.

His tracings came to a stop. His jaw clenched. We were at a dangerous precipice, and all I wanted was to throw myself off of it, regardless of the consequences. Would he jump with me?

When he spoke, his voice was lower. "Tell me."

My heart took off, pounding, trying to escape my chest.

"Most dreams were down by the water, sometimes in that front room against the door again, sometimes in your workshop. But one…" I hesitated, peeking up at him. How far did I want to go? *All the way,* something deep inside whispered. "One was about you and Rebecca and me."

His eyes widened, but he didn't back away. "What happened?"

I told him about the bedroom, about Rebecca on top of him, and even about the mix of jealousy and lust I felt as I watched. All the while I forced myself to keep my gaze on him, trying to read his expression. I couldn't decipher it. He was quiet after I finished. The longer I stood there in the still, dark room, the more restless I became. Had I gone too far?

"Is that something you're interested in?" he finally asked.

The question startled me. "You mean…for real?"

He nodded. Was he offering this or just clarifying? Edward was staring down at me, and a new kind of tension sparked between us, hot and unsteady, as my mind reeled through the question, again and again. I took a deep breath and tried to consider it. I thought about the flash of desire, that zing of jealousy as I watched this beautiful, mysterious woman pleasuring herself on Edward's cock. The scene turned me on, but was that what I *wanted*? Real life was much, much different than fantasy, as this summer kept trying to teach me. The real version of it would change things between Edward and me.

There is no Edward and me, I reminded myself—he had made that clear. It was off-limits, and he had held that line, more or less. I had yet to use one of my condoms, so in many people's eyes I was still a virgin, though what Edward had done to me against the cabin door felt too gloriously indecent not to count in my mind.

I wanted more, but I wanted it with him. In my handful of weeks here in Sweden, I'd rather have whatever this was with Edward. Even my first instinct—to wonder if he'd asked me this question because it's what he wanted—betrayed my true desire. Edward. It was a desire that left me vulnerable, a desire he'd turned away from. Still, I chose that one.

He was still watching me intently, his expression carefully bland, but his pulse ticked out a rapid beat at the base of his neck. What would it feel like to put my fingers on that vulnerable spot? Would it break his impervious façade? Instead, I met his gaze once again and tried for honesty.

"I don't want that," I said. "It's appealing as a fantasy, but that's not what I really want."

Edward let out a long breath, and it took a moment to understand it was relief that I saw on his face. His offer took on new meaning. Why had he asked if he wasn't interested?

"Have you done this before?" I asked. "You and Rebecca and someone else?"

He studied me.

"She's a fantastic mother," he said after a pause.

It was a strange thing to say, or at least I thought so at first. It took me a moment to register his point, that there were ideas about what made good mothers, and this was not one of them. I had my own opinions on mothers, formed in part by my sister's relationship with a married man, by the way she'd put Daisy aside for that man. Edward knew this. I'd told him about it that evening when we'd sat on his deck. I thought back to the day Sofia arrived, to the way Rebecca hugged her tightly, to the affection I'd seen.

"I saw their bond when Rebecca was here," I said.

Edward nodded. "People tend to read sexual preferences and acts as a commentary on their parenting. But they're very different things."

I considered Brenda again. Did she prefer married men, or did the guy she fell in love with happen to be married? Either way, should I fault her for that? It was true that Daisy seemed to come second for her, though she definitely loved her daughter… This was too much to sort out right now.

"I want to be clear that's not what went wrong between us," he continued in that clipped British accent. "Sofia was one of the few things that held us together."

I nodded. That part I understood.

"To answer your question, yes, I had—we had—threesomes." He was watching me carefully, like he was gauging my reaction. "She like to throw parties, all-night, bacchanalian parties with wine and food and sex. At first, I was very drawn in by it all. It was part of Rebecca's appeal."

I definitely understood her magnetic appeal. I had felt it the moment she entered the house. It was what drew me into her study and found its way into my dreams. That mix of curiosity, jealousy and desire returned as I pictured the dining room overflowing with fruits and meats and desserts, the raucous guests in various states of undress, seeking pleasure wherever they wanted to find it. And I saw Edward, standing at the head of the table, lording over the night. Was he at home in this scene, or did he keep his distance, just tasting. I imagined that the guests would be eager to find themselves in his bedroom.

Edward frowned a little, and it felt like he was farther away now.

"At first I got caught up in the pleasure of it," he continued, "and I thought maybe I'd escaped the kind of distant, stifling relationship my parents had. That stagnant hostility filled our house. It was part of why I refused to come with them the night of their deaths."

He paused, letting the sentence hang in the air, heavy with guilt, as I tried, unsuccessfully, to put these pieces together. *His parents' deaths.*

"Rebecca's parents ran in the same circles as mine, and they would have approved of her. It was one of the reasons I married her. But after a few years, our marriage felt just as distant and stifling as my parents'. And I started to wonder why I didn't mind sharing my wife. I can be a very possessive man."

His eyes flared with the heat from the first night together, reminding me of those moments when his gaze made me feel like I was the only thing on earth worth paying attention to. But when he spoke again, that heat turned to something else. "Rebecca pulled me out of a very dark time in my life, and I will always be grateful for that. But I don't feel the things with her that I want to feel about my wife. I wanted to untangle myself from my past, and I couldn't do it with Rebecca."

I was trying to process everything he'd said, but it was too much. I had seen hints of something dark lingering inside him. At first I'd imagined Rebecca at the center of the darkness, but maybe I should have known I was wrong all along. This wasn't a 1930's novel, where a fallen woman plays the evil villain. Something had wounded him deeply, and I wanted to know what it was. Despite the fact that I had no business prying into my boss's life, Edward was a mystery I couldn't stop trying to piece together.

"What kinds of things do you want to feel?" I asked.

Edward shook his head. "I'm not sure I'm capable of anything more than I gave Rebecca."

I frowned at him, refusing to believe it. The sentence came out even, almost unemotional, but I could hear the layers of pain and sadness he carried with him.

"Try, Edward. What do you want?"

He lifted his hand and brushed his fingers down my neck, over my collarbone. "Something different. Something so far from my past."

His words could have so easily come from my own lips. They held the desires I'd felt all summer, to experience something far enough away that my life didn't weigh me down. But I was far away from Brooklyn, and he was still at home, in this room in a house that echoed of the past he was trying to escape. There had been a hole in my life for so long, since my father left, or maybe it had been there all along. Did he have this hole in him, too? I'd staunched the flow of emotions with my fantasies, and it was never enough. But right now, with Edward's hand on my skin, each warm breath setting off new waves of heat.

"What do you want?" he asked.

I searched for a way to capture all these ideas that swirled inside me, creating a storm of lust and need and want. So much want. "I want something different, too, something that would change everything about the way I see the world."

Then I gave in. I stopped trying to resist and reached for him. I touched him the way I'd been aching to. I traced the line of his jaw, and I felt the bristle of his clean-shaven cheek on my fingers. I let my hand travel lower, over his chest and his stomach, but my gaze didn't leave his. I didn't want to miss anything, not the way his eyes grew heavy-lidded and sultry as my hand traveled lower, not the way his jaw tightened as I tugged the tails of his shirt from his trousers. I'd never used the word trousers before, but I'd never been this close to a man who dressed like this, as if clothes themselves had been invented just for him.

As I fingered the buttons of his shirt, his hand covered mine, and I tried to push away the disappointment that ran through me. I had known how this would go, didn't I?

"I know," I whispered. "Off-limits."

His eyes grew darker, as if those words turned him on, too. "What do you want tonight?"

My heart took off again. Was his self-control crumbling? "Whatever I can have with you."

He didn't move, and for a moment I thought he would leave me there. Maybe he was debating it. But then his lips were on mine, and all rational thoughts ended. All that existed was the softness of his lips, the stroke of his tongue. His hand swept across my cheek, and I was lost again in the slow, deep thrusts of his tongue. We kissed until I had forgotten where I was. The ache I had been trying to tamp down flared to life again, turning my insides to liquid. I needed him. This time I wasn't going to hold back.

An unwanted thought fluttered through my mind. How did I tell him I was a virgin? Or maybe I didn't tell him…

I focused on his buttons again. Even these were fancy, mother-of-pearl, and they slipped easily through the silk-soft material of his shirt. One, then another, his breaths came in rasps as I continued down until his shirt hung open, exposing a white undershirt. I took one of his hands and turned it over, brushing my fingers over his rough skin, exploring him the way he had done to me. I unfastened the first button of his cuff, then the second, exposing the vulnerable skin of his wrist. I touched the veins that pulsed under his skin, then reached for the other hand.

"I've wanted to touch you since the morning I found you in the library," I confessed as I slid his shirt over his shoulders. He shrugged it off, and it fell onto the floor. Then he tugged off the last layer, exposing miles of muscle and sun-kissed skin. I couldn't take my eyes from him, the two halves of him in front of me. The lower half was the reclusive, brooding man in luxurious trousers and leather shoes that were likely hand-stitched, just for him, but the top half belonged to the man I'd seen on the boat, free, maybe even happy. His eyes were heavy with desire, and his jaw was tight, as if these two sides of him warred inside. But I didn't want to see which would win. I wanted both.

I stared at his chest, over the hard muscles, the dusting of hair. His jaw worked, as if he was restraining himself, keeping himself in check, but he didn't move to stop me. I continued down, taking in everything, the heat, the scent of him, the way his stomach tightened at my touch. My hands drifted further, over the soft leather of his belt, over the grey fabric of his trousers, and I let my fingers linger on the hard length that pushed against it. Edward let out a groan, and his patience seemed to snap. His arms were around me, lifting me, my body pressed against his. I moaned in relief, but then he was gone, and I was perched on his desk.

"Lie down." His voice was a raspy growl, and I obeyed, resting my head on the leather blotter. Papers fluttered off the stack, but Edward didn't seem to notice. His gaze was fixed between my legs, so full of hunger. He slipped off my flats, then said, "Put your feet on my shoulders."

There was something in his voice, some mixture of authority and need that resonated deep inside, like he had dialed perfectly into the frequency my body ran on, a frequency I'd searched for but never quite found. Until now. It was playing so clearly, as if it was meant just for him.

"There's only one thing I regret about that first night when I tasted you," he said, his gaze dark.

"Drinking numbs me, and most of the time I want that. But not that night. And definitely not right now."

Something about that revelation felt important, but before I could process it, he pulled my panties aside, and I lost my mind. Pleasure blossomed, unfolded, building so quickly I didn't know how to contain it. I shook and writhed as he pleasured me. That first night in the cabin, he had experimented, finding the things I liked. This time, he remembered them, and they came together like a song on my body. The orgasm came fast, explosive, and I bit my hand to keep from screaming out my release. He brought me down softly, stroking, his breath heavy, setting off aftershocks inside.

At some point he shifted, moving my feet off his shoulders. I floated in the bliss as he stood up and walked to the other side of his desk. He bent to kiss me, then opened a drawer and pulled out a condom. My brain was moving slowly, and it took me a moment to remember. This was the point where I should tell him. If I was going to tell him.

I propped myself on my arms, trying to shake some sense into my brain. Right now felt so good, and I was wary of what would happen if I brought up the subject of virginity. Would he stop?

"I've never done this," I said quickly, before I could change my mind.

He stilled. The condom crackled in his hand, but I couldn't read his expression.

After a long, torturous pause, he asked, "Do you want to?"

"Very much. I…I just thought you should know."

He looked at me for a long time, intense but not awkward.

"Are you sure?"

"Definitely."

He didn't move, and disappointment flooded through me. Would he back away now? I met his gaze, letting him see how much I wanted him. Finally, he nodded. He unzipped his trousers, the sound triggering off a new ripple of pleasure and excitement. This was happening, and it felt so very real. I watched as he took himself out, full and hard, but before I could study his cock further, he was rolling down the condom.

"Don't you want to do this on a bed? Somewhere else instead of…" He tilted his chin, gesturing at his desk. But up against his desk in this old-fashioned study made this all the better. It felt both illicit and safe. Both wrong and right in the hottest sense.

His hand slid between my legs.

"I don't want to hurt you." His voice was strained. "You have to be wet for me."

That definitely wasn't a problem. We both groaned as he stroked me, sliding his fingers in, feeling the hot need inside me.

"Oh, yes." His words were tight, strained as I moved, grinding against his hand.

"Please," I begged. "I want more."

"Tell me how you're feeling." His hand disappeared, and his cock nudged against my entrance. A new burst of heat blossomed as he nudged again.

"So good." I could barely get out the words.

We both looked down, to where we were joining. It was almost unbearably erotic, so intimate. He pushed further. I was full, so full. The sensation was strange and new and overwhelming. *Oh.* The word was a sigh. Had I spoken it aloud? I no longer could tell.

He pushed again, a little harder this time, and then there was pain. My body froze. He must have felt my reaction because the pleasure I'd seen on his face turned to alarm. He cupped my head with his hand and pressed my cheek to his chest. I listened to his heartbeat, trying to relax. I don't know how long we stayed like that, taking long breaths, but gradually the pain lessened and there was only the fullness. Delicious fullness. I moved my hands to his hips and pulled him closer. Edward's breath caught, but he let me guide him, experimenting, first with small movements, then more. On the next thrust, he angled his hips up, and a bolt of newfound pleasure shot through me.

"Like that," I moaned. He took over, his hands grasping my hips, and he thrusted, thrusted. I reached for his chest, getting lost in the way his muscles moved, getting lost in the fullness of his cock, the pleasure that bloomed from that spot. His lips were parted, and his muscles strained. His strokes got harder.

"Yes." I panted and moaned and tried so hard to keep quiet, but it was impossible.

I reached between us and touched that spot he'd devastated with his mouth. The moment I touched it, another orgasm ran through me, a tidal wave, overtaking everything. Edward's hands tightened on my hips, and his thrusts were hard, and then he was holding me again, his groans in my ear, whispering something I didn't understand.

Chapter 8

"Where did all that money come from?"

I fumbled with my phone as my mother's voice splashed through the languid haziness of my half-asleep brain.

"It's three in the morning here, and I have no idea what you're talking about," I said thickly. "And hello. It's nice to talk to you too."

She ignored my sarcasm.

"The extra bonus," she said impatiently. "Practically Perfect Nannies called to make sure the transfer had gone through."

What? I sat up in bed, trying to clear my head. "But I—"

"You were right, Ava," she said, cutting me off. "I'm sorry I told you not to take this job. I was just worried you'd be traveling so far, but you were right. It does make a difference."

I wanted to tell her that I still had no clue what she was talking about, but how long had it been since I'd heard this excitement in her voice? I wasn't ready to hear this happiness disappear, so I probed carefully.

"What exactly did the person from the agency say?"

"Just that the client had asked for confirmation that we received it."

"I see," I hedged. "Can I call you later?"

"Yes, of course. I just wanted to tell you. We can pay off most of the credit card debt and maybe even go out to a fancy dinner."

Her soft laughter was from a distant past, and something tightened in my chest. Years ago, stress and worries had not yet consumed her. This was the mother I missed, the person I'd almost forgotten she could be.

"Thank you for calling, Mama."

I ended the call and stared out into my room, the last of sleep fading away. Sunlight glowed near the horizon, and the night was still. I rubbed my eyes, trying to think straight. Edward had made a payment last night, and I was guessing it happened after we'd had sex. Which sounded a hell of a lot like getting paid for sex.

I told myself that there could be another explanation, that I shouldn't jump to conclusions, but how could I not? I couldn't leave this alone. I got out of bed, and I didn't even know where I was headed until I was out of my room. His bedroom was off-limits, but so was what he had done.

The hallway was quiet. I passed the staircase and the door to the attic, trying to come up with alternative explanations. The farther I walked, the less certain I felt. If I opened his door for real, what would I find? I rested my hand on his knob, swallowed and turned it.

The door opened, and my gaze went straight to the bed. Unlike in my dream, it was large and modern, with lots of blue and white, and Edward lay in the middle, with his arm over his head. I took a few tentative steps forward. He looked so relaxed. Almost vulnerable. I wasn't prepared to feel this kind of tenderness for him, not after what he'd done. I tried to harden my heart.

"Edward?"

He didn't stir.

"Edward," I repeated, a little louder.

He opened his eyes, and his gaze went from sleepy to alarmed almost instantly. He bolted up to sitting. "Did something happen to Sofia?"

"Nothing's wrong with Sofia," I said quickly.

He lay back in bed, but now his chest was exposed, that beautiful chest I had traced with my fingers, the one I had watched as he thrust…. An unwanted bolt of heat ran through me, and I looked away.

Edward reached for his bedside clock. "It's just after three in the morning, Ava. Why are you awake?"

I supposed that was the polite version of asking why the hell I was in his room at this hour. I was invading his personal space. It was one of the few limits he'd set in this house, and I had just crashed right through it. He didn't sound angry, not exactly. Just wary.

I steadied myself and continued. "I just got a call from my mother, who said a large sum of money was deposited into our account."

He nodded, and the lack of surprise on his face confirmed all of my suspicions.

"You paid me after last night."

He nodded again, like the connection between these two was obvious to him. My stomach churned. On the way over to his room, I had tried to convince myself that Edward wouldn't pay his nanny for sex. But he had just confirmed that this was no coincidence, and worse, he couldn't see why I might have a problem with this. What the hell?

There was nothing wrong with sex workers, but it required a clear arrangement, laid out there from the beginning, clear to *both* parties. Our understanding was different, or at least I thought it was. All those wants he had mentioned the night before, his craving for something new, something far from the past—was this what he meant?

Edward sat up again, scrubbed his hands over his face, then studied me carefully. "You look angry."

"Of course I'm angry," I spat out. "I didn't have sex with you for money."

Now he did look surprised, which was rich.

"In case no one in your upper-class life has told you," I said with a sweeping arm, gesturing around his room, not hiding my distain, "That's the kind of arrangement you let someone know about beforehand. Not after. Because I was under a very different understanding."

Edward's eyes were wide. He looked stunned. Life had certainly insulated him if he was shocked. And still, *still*, my mind was stubborn, unable to fit together the Edward that had kissed me and held me in the most tender way last night and the Edward who had paid me for my time.

"I didn't pay you for sex, Ava." His voice was firm and hard. The last of the sleep was gone from his face, and he looked so serious, more serious than I had ever seen him. He raked a hand through his hair. "This was a bonus for getting Sofia to speak."

"Oh." I blinked, taking in this statement. That made more sense…but he could have waited until the next morning.

"But why did you stay up last night to do it? You could have waited until today or just told me before I left your study, but you didn't."

He let out a sigh. "You're right. I suppose the sex did factor in, but not in the way you're thinking."

I crossed my arms and eyed him warily.

"Last night created a risk for you. You took this job for money, and I'm the person who decides whether you get the bonus. I wanted to take away some of your risk, to free you to make your own choices with me. What happened last night makes that more complicated. I don't want you to be in the position where you make personal decisions because of a business agreement, so I did this to take money off the table for us." He paused, watching me closely. "Last night got very…personal."

Tears welled in my eyes, and I turned away in embarrassment. How naïve I'd been to think that this thing with Edward would be so simple. How naïve that I assumed it could be about pleasure and connection, but somehow I could avoid getting invested. This little incident exposed how much more I wanted from him, how much I already cared. My deepest fantasy had become real. I was intimately involved with my boss. What I hadn't expected was how easily and quickly it could hurt. I knew this would only get more dangerous the longer I stayed here.

I pulled myself together and turned to meet his gaze again. "You should have asked first."

"If I had, would you have said yes, or would you have made this about the connection between the money and the sex?"

I would have, and he knew it, too. "In a personal relationship, it's my right to say no to things, even if you disagree with my choice."

He was silent for a moment. He looked out the window, out into the brightness of the Swedish night.

"I did it for me too," he finally said. He didn't look at me, and I could see the strain in his expression. It was taking a lot for him to say this. "If I didn't, then I would wonder if money was part of this."

He gestured between us. I blinked, a little stunned. My first instinct was to be offended, that he was implying I'd sleep with him because of his money. That's what it sounded like on my side, at least, but there was so much vulnerability in his voice that I tried to hold judgement. I wanted to tell him that his wealth wasn't a factor, but was that true? Of course, I wasn't after his money in any direct way, but my attraction to authority figures was about power, and money was a form of power. This idea was uncomfortable and messier than I wanted it to be. It was probably messy for Edward, too. Could I really fault him for trying to manage it, the way I was? I took a deep breath and sat down on his bed. He turned to me, and I couldn't read his expression.

"This is probably why people are advised not to sleep with their employees," I said.

He huffed out a little laugh, then shook his head. "I'm so sorry, Ava."

Earlier in his study, I thought about all the ways we connected, but wealth was something that separated us, and both our ineffective attempts to ease each other's worries were signs that the gap between us was wide. Maybe this should be a wake-up call to stop before I got even more hurt.

"I can't pretend to understand your position," I finally said. "But please don't do something like that again without talking to me first."

"I won't."

I smiled a little. "Though you did make my mother very happy."

He didn't look especially pleased. "I was hoping to make you happy, too."

The words tumbled inside me, stirring up emotions I didn't want to feel for him. I looked away. As the silence settled between us, it occurred to me once again that I was in his room. I had spent the last few weeks imagining all sorts of things, and now I could finally look around. His room was a larger and fancier version of mine, which I supposed made sense considering we were at mirror ends of the house. There was an arched doorway that joined this room with the one next to it, and both rooms were decorated much in the same style, old-fashioned charm mixed with more modern pieces. There was a sitting area in front of the French doors, about the size of my apartment's living room, with an armchair, a sofa, and a coffee table. The stack of newspapers on the table suggested he used the space frequently. I could picture Edward sitting there, lord of the manor house, with his coffee and his newspaper, looking out the doors at the expanse of his grounds.

I scanned the rest of the room but came to a stop at the wall behind where I was sitting. Two things that stood out. One was a rather small portrait of a family. It wasn't of Rebecca nor Sofia, but I was almost sure the boy was Edward, with his dark and stunning blue eyes.

But unlike the Edward that I knew, that boy's smile was so carefree it made my heart ache. Also pictured were his parents and a sister, I assumed. The parents looked cool, distant, not so far from the look Edward often wore, but the sister had Edward's smile. This was the first trace of his family I'd seen, and I wanted to know who they were and why this was my first glimpse.

The second thing that surprised me was an old-fashioned rolling service tray. On the top level were bottles of liquor, lots of them. Even that wouldn't have stood out in a house like this except for two things. First of all, the bottles were all identical, like they were purchased for the world's most single-minded party. Second, on the tray underneath, there was only one glass. All this liquor was just for him.

How often did he sit in his armchair, drinking by himself? His stern directive not to venture into this wing of the house was taking on new meaning.

"It looks bad," he said, and his voice was hard.

Heat rose to my cheeks, and I felt like he had caught me snooping just as I stumbled onto something very intimate. Now I couldn't back away.

"I don't drink every day," he continued. "I don't drink when I'm in charge of Sofia. I'm afraid something might happen and I wouldn't hear her."

I was very glad that he had thought about that part.

"It's just when no one else is here," he added.

The statement was another missing piece of the puzzle I'd been trying to solve. That first day I'd arrived made sense now, the dark circles under his eyes, the whiff of alcohol. He had been in the middle of a bender, and I had interrupted it. "That's why you were so angry when I showed up early."

I said it more to myself, but he answered anyway.

"I wouldn't say I was angry, more irritated. I didn't want anyone in the house, and certainly not someone so…" He frowned and didn't finish the sentence. As much as I wanted to know how that sentence ended, I didn't push him.

"I'm sorry I invaded your privacy." The apology was for both that first day and for tonight.

But Edward just shrugged. "It's probably better you know. I understand it's a problem, but I haven't been ready to stop."

We sat in silence, our gazes locked. He seemed to be waiting for something from me. Judgement? I couldn't muster any of that. I knew I should probably be feeling shock or hesitation or something, but all I could feel right now was sadness. He was suffering, and I was almost sure the portrait was somehow part of that pain. I couldn't pretend like I understood when I knew so little about him, but I understood grief. I'd lost my father in all ways that counted, and there were ways I'd lost my mother when he left as well.

"Do you want me to leave?" I asked.

"No. But you're free to go."

"I'd rather be here."

I lifted the covers and crawled in beside his warm body, and he turned to lie next to me. He urged me onto my side so I wasn't facing him, then wrapped his arm around me.

"You can ask me more about it if you want," he said after a while.

I wasn't even sure where to begin. "Does Rebecca know?"

"Yes. It's one of the reasons we split. She wanted me to quit, and I didn't want to." He paused then added, "She knew how careful I was about Sofia, so that wasn't her worry."

I could see why it would still be hard.

"There were plenty of other reasons too," she said he added, his voice harder now. "We barely saw each other, just trading off time at home with Sofia or leaving her with the nanny so we could both go off on separate vacations."

I couldn't imagine this life, so I didn't try. Instead, I asked, "Do you want to quit drinking?"

He let out a slow breath. "When I drink, I want to quit. I tell myself this is the last time. But when I'm sober, I don't want to quit anymore. What's waiting for me at the other end of it?"

The statement was depressing as hell. I thought about the days and weeks and even years after my father left, the emptiness that lingered in the spaces he used to fill. There were times the emptiness took over. But through those times I'd leaned on Ruthie, on my mother, even on Brenda. Who did he lean on?

I couldn't stay all night, wrapped in his arms. But right now, I was here, and it made everything a little better. Did it have the same effect on him?

"You have the boats," I said after a while.

"I do."

"And Sofia."

"Yes, Sofia." His voice was soft.

And you have me.

"Maybe that means it's time to rethink what's waiting for you?"

He pulled me closer. "Maybe."

Chapter 9

After that night, I no longer resisted the urge to go to Edward, and he welcomed me without reservation. Some nights he'd ask me questions about my life and family, which he found fascinating for reasons I couldn't understand. But other nights were silent except for the sounds of the pleasure and relief our bodies found in each other. I assumed the urgency would fade, but instead it seemed to grow with each night. I wanted more.

I should have left it at that. I knew I should just let us be together like this for this limited time, but I couldn't. It felt as if we had both come to each other lost, both hiding away from the world in our own ways. He was lost in some hidden sorrow from his past, and I had been drifting through my life, lost in my fantasies. But the revelations of that first night I came to his bedroom stayed with me, and I knew all those things simmered beneath his surface. I found myself checking the levels of his bottles. I couldn't forget the drinking, even if I never saw evidence of it.

After a few surreptitious glances, he asked, "Does it make you uncomfortable?"

I thought about the question, then shook my head. "Just sad."

I couldn't help but think the bottles were as much a self-inflicted punishment as they were a comfort. But it wasn't my business. I was leaving soon, so soon.

I tried not to count down the days. Sofia and I were growing closer in new ways now that she spoke, now that I could hear her thoughts, though she was still quiet. She seemed like a confident reader in Swedish, so I figured we could start a little on English. We had read the books I had bought enough times that she probably knew most of them by heart, so I figured they would be a good start.

"Do you know what this first line says?" I asked.

She looked down at the page for a moment, studying it, then looked back up at me and nodded.

"Excellent," I said.

She didn't seem to want to read aloud, so I improvised. "How about I trace the words while I read them, and you can follow along? Then, when I'm not here, you can still read this by yourself."

This seemed to work. We filled our time with books and walks and toys and games. Both Sofia and Edward invited me to sail with them many times. As much as I wanted to feel that rush again, that freedom of my first ride, I turned them down. It was their time together.

"I'll go another day," I said, though we all knew my days were quickly disappearing. Instead I watched them from the beach, listening to their voices echo off the water as they disappeared into the shimmering Baltic.

When they returned, Sofia and I stayed at the beach to build villages and castles in the sand. Sometimes Edward lingered, watching, though he never joined. In the evenings, I listened to their voices at supper, reminding me that I was an outsider, not part of this family.

I could have sworn that the forest whispered the same message. I spent many free hours wandering the paths, to the trees, breathing in their scents, but I could have sworn the paths played tricks on me, rearranging themselves when I turned my back. Was the forest telling me I was only allowed to walk here as long as I remembered my place? That this privilege could easily be revoked?

Britt-Marie was less circumspect. I was sure she knew about Edward and me, though I didn't know how. We tried to be careful, but her snubs turned to glares as the weeks passed.

"I think Britt-Marie hates me," I said one night.

She doesn't like me much these days, either. Not since I left Rebecca."

He left her? I'd assumed it was the other way around.

"Why doesn't Britt-Marie quit?" I asked.

"She stays for Sofia. She has a thing about broken homes and she's afraid Sofia will suffer because of it."

"And you still want her here?" It seemed strange to employ someone who actively disliked him, no matter how good her food was or how nicely she put Sofia to bed.

Edward looked out the window. "She's been part of this family for most of my life."

She was a part of his past, the past that I was sure haunted him. But this suggested he also clung to it, and I wanted to know why. I told myself I would ask later, whenever that was.

As the days floated by, I could feel myself falling for him. I took a stack of books down to the living room where I'd sat the first day I arrived. It was at the center of the house, impossible to miss if Edward wandered through the halls. He did, lingering more often when he came upon Sofia and me. Then one day as we read on the sofa, Edward came to a stop next to us. I could feel the tension coming off with him, but I just kept reading. We finish the book, and I was almost sure he would leave, but Sofia said something to him in Swedish. He said nothing for a long time. Sofia looked up at him, waiting. Finally, he sat on the sofa. Sofia climbed onto his lap.

"Can you read the *Snowy Day* story, please?" she asked me.

"Of course."

As I read, I watched them out of the corner of my eye. Sofia found Edward's hand and pulled it around her waist, then put hers on top of it. She seemed to sense this was hard for him, and it made me wonder how much she knew about her own family.

The closer my departure date came, the more difficult it was not to think about the future. No matter how hard I tried, the future kept intruding, reminding me of all the things I'd never get to do. At night, when I lay restless in the eternal twilight, I tried to fall back into my fantasy world, to play out future scenarios in my head, but reality intruded in ways it never used to.

I believed Edward genuinely cared for me, so when I left, we might even promise to see each other again. But our lives were so different, and frankly, I didn't want him coming to our little building in Brooklyn, to see the run-down apartment that we had all worked so hard to keep. I didn't want to see the surprise on his face when the class differences sunk in, and I didn't want to explain why my mother, even if she had all the money in the world, wouldn't leave that place. Actually, that might be the only part he did understand.

Sometimes I hoped Edward would offer to extend my stay, that I could become his full-time nanny for the year. But even in my fantasy world, this didn't work. It was one thing to fall into sleeping with him, but negotiating a new contract, knowing that the arrangement probably involved sex? I didn't think I could handle that.

I'd also imagined that he'd proposed to me on my last day. The idea had a fairytale appeal to it, of course, though even that scenario was filled with hurdles I couldn't ignore. First, I couldn't abandon my mother and Brenda financially, and leaving them, leaving New York, was too much to consider, no matter how much I loved the tranquility of Sweden. Second, though this house was more luxurious and extravagant than anything I would likely set foot into, living here was quite another issue. I was a foreigner in this house, and I would never be fully welcomed, not by the house, not by the forest and definitely not by Britt-Marie. The flame between Edward and me kept that feeling at bay, but it still lurked in the shadows. The hardest part was seeing the past on Edward's face when I caught him unaware. I didn't know if I could live like that, watching the sadness that seem to seep into him every day. And then there was the drinking. It felt connected to that sadness, a part of him that was separate from me, a part that connected him to his old life.

If this was a fairytale, it was the original, more ominous version. I was bursting to talk to Edward about everything on my mind, but my self-preservation instincts were stronger. I knew I was going home in a few weeks, and I knew we'd be saying goodbye in one way or another. One way or another, this was going to end.

There was nowhere more difficult to forget about the future than in Edward's bedroom. I never slept there.

I never wanted to run the risk of oversleeping and returning from Edward's room in front of Sofia and Britt-Marie, but I found reasons to stay longer and longer. Edward didn't bring up the subject. He also never came to my room, and one night I worked up the courage to mention it.

"This has to be your choice," he said as he positioned himself over me, his shoulders flexing under the weight of his body. "If I came to you whenever I wanted..."

His voice trailed off, and he shook his head, as if to say I wouldn't want whatever that would mean. But I did. I constantly wanted to brush my lips against his and feel the weight of his body on mine. He tasted of salt water like he always did, and as I put my mouth to his skin, I wondered if I would forever think of him when I went to the beach.

There was still so much I didn't know. As my departure neared, I grew bolder, asking more questions.

"How long has this house been in your family?"

"My great-grandfather built it over one hundred years ago. He made his money in shipping." The answer wasn't a surprise, but his tone was flat and almost detached. I guess I had expected some sort of pride in his voice, but I didn't hear any. "My job is to make sure his fortune keeps growing and our family name lives on."

It was a strange purpose in life, almost impersonal, like Edward could be replaced by anyone as long as they grew the family fortune. I wonder if the same thought had occurred to him.

"First my great-grandfather bought the property, and then he built the cabin, the one attached to my workshop by the water. When he had amassed more money, the construction of this house started. It took nine years. My great-grandmother passed away before they had the chance to move in, and he spent his last years here alone. The house was what he'd worked for. He wanted his family name to last. And it has."

His great-grandfather seemed like the type who would have had a portrait painted of him at some point, and I wondered again why there wasn't one hanging somewhere in the house.

"Do you like living here?" I suppose it was a strange question to ask, considering the fact that he likely had the money to live anywhere, and he'd chosen to be here. Still, I didn't sense that the answer was straightforward.

"Sometimes the place feels haunted, like my great-grandfather is still here, reminding me of my duty to the family name." He gave a wry laugh. "Sounds a little far-fetched, doesn't it?"

"Not at all." I thought about all the times the house had felt alive when I walked through the halls.

"All I want to do is be on my own and work on boats. Rebecca says I'm not thinking enough about Sofia. That I should honor the family name, even if I don't want it. That it's her legacy, not just mine. She's right. And sometimes I wonder if this is my only connection with my daughter."

"No," I said quietly. "It's so much more than that."

The room was silent. I took a deep breath and asked the question I couldn't stop thinking about. "Can you tell me about your parents?"

He shook his head slowly. "Not now."

"When?"

"Before you leave."

Then he kissed me, a long, slow, intoxicating kiss. I was sure this was an attempt to distract me, and it worked. I was thoroughly, utterly distracted. I kissed him back, running my hands over his chest, over his arms, losing myself in the warmth of his body, in the way his fingers tightened around my hips and pulled me against him, until there was no future. There was no past. It was just the two of us, connected again.

His hands glide it up my thighs, under my dress and over my rear, like he couldn't get enough of me. He gripped me harder, like he was going to lift me, but I moved his hands away. I knelt in front of him and looked up into his eyes. There was warning mixed with the dark heat crackling in his gaze.

He swallowed. He was a man of few words, a man used to doing things his own way, and he seemed to be waging some kind of debate as to how to handle this situation. I smiled and let my hands travel up his thighs, until they were right next to the thick cock pressing against his trousers.

He'd gone down on me night after night, making me cry and beg for his mouth again and again, but I hadn't tried this yet. It was unbearably erotic in my mind, but I'd hesitated, and Edward hadn't pushed. I suspected it might not be something I'd actually like in practice, mostly because it was what my first boss had wanted from me. Would it feel the same with Edward?

"Do you like this?" I asked softly.

"*Gud*, yes," he rasped.

I pulled the strap of his leather belt through the loop, unfastening it first, then his trousers. I eased down his zipper. Just this simple act was turning me on like a lighthouse, and my body pulsed with flashes of desire, calling to him. He led out a soft hiss as I ran my fingers under the waistband of his boxers, my heart pounding in my chest. He had dedicated himself to my pleasure whenever we were together. What did he want? I wanted to get it just right.

"Tell me how you like it," I whispered.

He let out something between a groan and a laugh. "Anything you do I'll like. I could probably come just like this, with you on your knees, looking up at me like you want to please me."

The pleasure of those words was almost too much. This was what I wanted. He smelled like the sea and sex, like heaven.

"I want to please you," I answered. "Very much."

"You already do. Everything about you pleases me very much."

These words were the ultimate satisfaction. They poured through my body, filling every crack of uncertainty, covering every well-hidden thought that I wasn't enough. That if I wasn't so awkward, if I had been more attentive or well behaved or *something*, I would have pleased my father. Maybe he wouldn't have left. Maybe our lives would have been easier. But tonight, those feelings dissolved. Tonight I was good enough. Tonight Edward wanted me, just the way I was.

He let out a harsh breath. "Do you want this? Do you want to suck my cock?"

His words were taunting me. *He* was taunting me. I had watched him stroke himself one night while he went down on me, and now I understood. I couldn't believe how much pleasure I was getting from this. It wasn't better in my fantasies, like so many other things. The scent of him, the way my heart was trying to burst out of my chest—this was better right now. This was happiness.

Pre-cum was leaking out of his tip. I leaned down and licked it off.

"Yes," he hissed, so I ran my tongue over his head again. He took an audible breath, and a bolt of pleasure shot through me. I loved watching his face, that naked pleasure that crossed it. Pleasure that I was giving him. I was doing this. I fit my mouth over his head, and his eyes rolled back.

"You have the best mouth. I've been thinking about it since you walked into my house," he rasped.

How did he know exactly what to say? His stoic exterior had crumbled, and he was showing me all his wants, his cravings. They were for me. The thought was a giddy jolt of freedom. I slid my mouth over him, caressing his cock with my lips, and his hands traveled into my hair, not quite guiding, just feeling, caressing, as if he was reaching for more of me. So I sucked him in and pulled out again and again, getting lost in the dizzy excitement of giving him the pleasure he wanted.

"Yes, yes." His voice was deep and broken.

The more I pleasured him, the more the words came, a mixture of Swedish and English like he was forgetting himself, losing himself in this moment.

"I'm going to come, Ava," he bit out. "Open for me."

So I did. I took everything he gave me as his body jolted and tightened under me. He pulled out of my mouth and slumped onto his bed, as if his legs had given out on him. I looked up, and he was staring down at me with glassy-eyed wonder. I felt that wonder too.

He tugged on my hands, helping me to standing, then pulled me toward him. We collapsed onto his bed, a tangle of arms and legs and half-shed clothing. Edward was smiling at me. *Smiling*. I flashed to the man who had opened the door that first day, with his wild hair and eyes dark enough to make me shudder. Right now he looked so alive, and I thought how strange it was that a person was capable of such darkness and such lightness. That our capacity for great sadness and happiness existed so close together seemed impossible, and yet here it was true. And I thought back to myself, timidly stepping through his door that first day. That woman felt so far away. Now I was lying with Edward like it was the most natural thing.

Then Edward was kissing me again, and those ideas faded. All that was left was his touch. We fumbled with our clothes until we were both naked, skin to skin. I lay on top of him and pleasured myself against his cock, letting my nipples drag over the hard contours of his chest. He handed me a condom, and I rolled it on as he watched, then guided myself down his length in the way that I wanted. His eyes were hazy and dark, and he was completely focused on me.

"You are so lovely, Ava," he whispered.

His words reverberated deep inside, and I felt as though he was telling me something big, something that reached far beyond the pleasure of this moment. I moved faster, shifting to make a little space between us, searching for my clit. Edward gently brushed my hand away and took over, pleasuring me as I pleasured myself up and down his cock until I was drowning in ecstasy. I had to bite my lip to keep from calling for him, but the impulse was too strong. I cried his name, and he held on, watching me, until he followed, groaning as he jerked out his own orgasm, sending hot echoes of pleasure through my body. I slumped onto his chest, listening to the steady thump of his heart, feeling his warm, salty skin against mine. It felt like home.

Chapter 10

It wasn't just Edward that I dreaded leaving. I didn't want to leave Sofia. I had nannied before, but it was different this time, maybe because I was living with them, or maybe it was different because it was Sofia. Probably both. But I found myself searching for a little ways to keep in touch with her.

The day before I was supposed to leave, we were sitting on the beach, digging a hole as deep as we could, building a mountain range to surround us. The water was seeping into the hole from the bottom, slowing our progress significantly, but Sofia didn't seem to mind.

"Would you like me to write letters to you after I leave?" I asked.

She nodded, smiling up at me. "You can draw pictures for me."

"Of course. And I bet you'll be able to read the letters by yourself."

"Pappa can help me too."

I took a deep breath, trying to tamp down the emotion that this statement had the power to stir in me. "And if you have a picture you'd like to send me, I would love that, too."

She tilted her head a little, the way she did when she was considering something. Then she crawled over the sand and put her arms around me. She wasn't generally affectionate, at least not with me, so it took me by surprise. But I wrapped my arms around her and pulled her onto my lap. We sat like that, silently hugging, and when she looked up at me, her eyes welled with tears.

"I'll miss you, Sofia," I whispered in her ear.

She lay her head on my shoulder and held me tighter, and I never wanted to let her go.

That afternoon, a storm rolled in. The breeze turned cold, and Sofia spent the afternoon on my lap in her bedroom, drawing pictures and reading. By nightfall, the rain was coming down in heavy sheets, cloaking the endless sun in a heavy grey fog. I watch the rain from my bedroom window, wrapped in a sweater and leggings. I ate supper in the chair in the corner of my room, curled into a ball under the blanket. The windows were closed, so instead of listening to the musical lilt of Sofia's and Edward's Swedish, I thought about the night that was coming. Time had run out. Edward couldn't put off my questions any longer.

I asked to put Sofia to bed that night. We read for a long time, and when I was getting ready to leave, she asked when I was coming back to Sweden.

"I don't know. But I hope to someday."

Maybe she could hear the hesitation in my voice, but she didn't press me further. I kissed her forehead and tucked her in, trying not to think about the idea of never seeing her again. The sound of the rain echoed through the dark hallway as I made my way past the door to the attic. All summer I had wondered what lay up those stairs, but the creaks and groans of the house made me wonder if it was wise to probe. It's just a house, I reminded myself. I continued down the hallway and came to a stop in front of Edward's bedroom door. I took a deep breath and turned the brass knob.

The room was dark, lit by a single lamp next to his bed. Edward sat on the armchair facing the French doors, looking out into the darkness. He turned to me, and his expression was full of want and something else, something that tugged at the deepest parts of me, the parts I tried so hard to protect. But he exposed them. He exposed me. It should have scared me away, but instead I wanted to drown myself in this feeling with him. Edward crossed the room, his eyes dark and intense. I could feel hunger radiating off him, but his touch was gentle. He threaded one hand into my hair and brushed his lips over mine.

I let out a sigh and kissed him, tasting him as the wind howled outside. I knew I could get lost in this kiss, in his arms, in his body for the rest of the night if I wasn't careful. So I pulled away and looked up at him.

"You're very distracting."

He smiled. "I was thinking the same thing. But I don't mind being distracted."

I bit my lip. "Then I'll never get to ask my questions about you."

His smile faded, and he nodded. He took my hand and led me to the sofa and sat, sprawled out like a king, with one arm resting along the back. He motioned for me to sit too, and when I did, he wrapped his arm around me, pulling me closer, against his chest. We sat there for a long time, looking out into the darkness, and I might have sat there like that for the whole night, the attraction humming between us.

"What do you want to know?"

I tried to ask my question as gently as I could. "What happened to the rest of your family?"

I wanted to see his face, to see if that cool, detached look was back, but he held me against him.

"It happened when I was nineteen, just before I was supposed to start at university. Like most nineteen-year-olds, I was done with living at home and ready to get away. We lived in Stockholm, in the house where Rebecca lives now, and this was our summer home. My parents wanted me to come here for the last few weeks, before I left. Our family wasn't particularly close, but we had traditions that were sacred, and this was one of them. But I refused. I wanted to do the stupid kinds of things most nineteen-year-old boys want to do, not spend a couple weeks with my family. So after a big lecture about me not living up to my role in the family, I walked out. Just left.

"The accident happened on the way here to this house, on the two-lane road right off the highway. It was a drunk driver, which is uncommon here in Sweden. My parents were killed instantly. My younger sister…"

His voice trailed off, and I could hear how much pain this was bringing him. He took a deep breath and continued.

"My sister survived for a few weeks. She was in a coma, but I read to her anyway. I was there every day. She was all I had left, and there was nothing I could do except read her favorite books to her and beg her to live. She didn't."

I was frozen now, listening to this awful story, stunned by the pain he must have felt.

"It was all over the papers, of course. You expect this kind of publicity when you come from a high-profile family, but I couldn't deal with it. I didn't go to school that fall. I was a mess. Lots of drinking." He paused, letting me make the connection. "After a while, when I did pick myself up, I could feel the way people looked at me. Like I was naked, like every single thing inside me was exposed."

The hurt in his voice was so raw, so present. He had been living with this devastation since he was nineteen. I didn't realize I was crying until warm tears fell on my cheeks.

"So I went to England to study. And it felt good to just get away. I didn't forget, of course, but I guess I was learning to live with it."

I tried to imagine him there, all alone in a new country, trying to shut out the past.

"And then I met fun, wild Rebecca. Being with her felt like moving away from my past. But when we had Sofia, it all came back."

I tried to wipe away my tears surreptitiously, but he shifted to meet my gaze. He looked surprised.

"Hey, it was okay," he said quietly. "It sounds worse than it was."

I knew he was lying. I knew he was saying this because he could see the devastation in my face. But I could see the same in his, too.

"It's hard to know what to do when families are open wounds," I said. "They just never seem to heal, do they?"

I said it like it was a statement, but I wanted it to be a question. I wanted so badly not to know the answer that we both knew, that open wounds in families never did heal. Even after years of trying to put it behind him, his pain had come back with vengeance. I had covered mine up with enough cheeriness that no one even thought to ask, and he had done the opposite, buried himself so far away, living with the pain, wrestling with it, trying to find a way not to drag his daughter down with him.

Everything about Edward and me was different, but I understood this part of him. I knew what it was like for my own family to fall apart, and his loss was so much greater. It hurt to watch my mother work until her body ached, just to keep our apartment, but she was still here. My sister was still here. Edward had been alone in his survival.

Edward was still looking at me, studying my face in a way that he had before, like he was seeing me, but this time I didn't feel self-conscious. This time it actually felt good to have someone see me, someone who might understand. Someone who wouldn't see my life like a crash on the highway, thinking *I'm glad it wasn't me*. Someone who wouldn't see my sorrow as a reminder of how they wanted their world to stay in place.

But tomorrow, he would be someone in my past.

"So now you know," he said softly.

"Why didn't you tell me before?"

But I guess I already knew his answer. His words still echoed inside me, so close to my own. He wanted something different, something so far from his past.

"Self-preservation, I suppose," he finally said. There were hints of humor in his voice now. "What other questions should I brace myself for?"

I was still trying to process that first answer. If this were any other night, I would have stopped here. But tomorrow I was leaving. If I wanted to understand him, understand this place, this was my last chance.

"Will you show me what's in the attic?"

I turned to him, and his expression suggested he knew this question was coming. It took a moment for him to answer, and in that moment I was sure he was going to refuse, but he nodded. He stood, and I followed him across the room and out into the hallway. This was it. I'd been waiting to see what he kept in the attic since the first day. I still didn't have a clue what I would find.

Edward came to a stop in front of the attic door, resting his hand on the old brass knob, this one dull with disuse. He met my gaze, his eyes filled with that wariness that I had seen so many times this summer. His body hummed with tension, and I longed to reach for him. But he looked away and turned the knob, and the door swung open. I took a step. Another step. The stairs creaked and groaned their warnings, and the house shuddered in the storm. It was dark, the only light peeking through the curtains that covered the dormer windows. Heavy drops of rain pelted the glass, and a flash of lightening cast an eerie glow across the room.

Edward flipped a switch, lighting up the place. The third floor stretched the length of the house, but it was much narrower. My first thought was that it looked like the hall of a museum, the Vallenberg Museum, a dusty, deserted tribute to the family. Between the windows, the walls were covered with portraits of people, relatives I assumed, in various styles of dress. I had been right about his great-grandfather being a portrait kind of man. There was maritime memorabilia, anchors and iron spikes along one wall and painted wood statues of women and sea monsters that looked like they could have sat on the front of a boat. But what I found myself staring at were the giant model ships on pedestals throughout the room, incased in glass. Did Edward build these?

The ships drew me in. They were incredible, the tiny, intricate pieces, the way they fit together. Edward followed me around as I inspected one, then another, standing just behind me like a patient museum guide.

"Who built this?"

"My father and I did. Together." Aside from the small portrait in Edward's bedroom, there was no evidence of his father in the rest of the house. And yet there was a whole floor of reminders collecting dust up here. I didn't quite understand this, but other pieces were falling into place.

"This was where you learned about boats," I whispered. "From your father."

He gave me a little smile. "That and engineering school."

I nodded, but what I meant was his love of boats. This had been his connection to his father. And now he was trying to pass it on to Sofia.

"Does Sofia know about this room?"

"Of course. But she's not very interested in models of boats or old portraits." He was wearing a wry smile, but the sadness was in his eyes. He was the last link to the memories in this room. Was that why he lived in this gloomy house?

"She loves sailing," I said.

"I'm pleased with that. Very pleased."

I didn't know what to think of this room, this monument to his past. Once again, it struck me how alone he seemed.

"Is it hard to see these things?"

"I moved here, the way the first Vallenberg son of each generation is supposed to, but I left Rebecca, something that would have made my father furious. Every day I try to remember my duty to my family while trying to forget my past. You can see my problem."

"So you moved these memories up here to the attic?"

"Sometimes it felt like they were taunting me." He gave a humorless laugh. "Sounds a little crazy."

"Not at all."

"Also, Rebecca hates all this stuff. She thinks it makes the house look stuffy." Edward shook his head. "I've tried to follow the path that was expected of me. I've tried to scrub this house clean of the loss memories, but it doesn't work."

I didn't know what to say. His body had been drawn tight with tension since he'd laid his hand on the doorknob, and now that we were here, the tension shifted into something else. I turned to face him, and his gaze traveled down my body in blatant interest. He didn't want my words. He wanted a different kind of consolation.

"I want you."

His words were both a demand and a plea, and then he lowered his mouth to mine. He kissed like he was hungry, like he couldn't get enough of me. I kissed him back, threading one hand through his hair. His hands found their way under my sweater and slid over my skin. They were rough, calloused from the tools he worked with, the wood he handled, and the friction made my breath catch. Then he was lifting me, lowering me to the cool wooden floor. He tore off his shirt, then lifted my sweater over my head. His hands moved to the clasp of my bra, baring my breasts to him. He held himself over me, his warm chest skimming over my nipples, and his eyes heavy, intense. I spread my thighs wider, pressing against his thick cock. He rested on one elbow, and his other hand traveled down, over my hips and around my rear, squeezing. His tongue was waging a slow, sensual assault on my mouth until nothing else mattered except his taste, his touch. I wanted to be closer. I *had* to be closer. It felt like he was worshiping me, right here in the middle of this shrine to his family, and all I could think of was how much I wanted that. I wanted everything.

His gaze traveled down to my breasts. I had never dreamed how sensitive my nipples could be. He toyed with one, then sucked on it while his big hand played with the other, kneading, caressing, squeezing until I couldn't think. I was rubbing my core against his length, driving myself further toward ecstasy. His groans were primitive as I explored the muscles of his biceps, of his back. We were skin against skin, his long, warm body resting against mine. When we were like that, I felt safe, like I could let go and the world wouldn't cave in around me.

He fumbled with my leggings, and I lifted my hips as he slid my very last layers away. I was naked before him on the hardwood floor of this strange attic, and somehow, it felt right.

He lowered his trousers and slid on a condom, then wrapped his arms around me, holding me close. He slid into me. Oh, the pleasure, the relief of this fullness inside me. His breaths were short staccatos in my ear as he held me against him. Then he started to move. His long, hard strokes, the angle of his hips, the sensation building deep within fueled my pleasure. Every rasp of his breath created a new spark. I closed my eyes, losing myself as he thrusted, thrusted until my orgasm came. With one last, shuttering breath, he howled out his pleasure, thrusting over and over.

I panted under his heavy body, losing myself in his warmth as the aftershocks faded. He rolled to his side, taking me with him. We were face to face, and his eyes were dark and magnetic. I couldn't look away. We stared at each other, and slowly the satisfaction I'd seen on his face faded.

"You're leaving tomorrow." His statement was flat, and his mouth twisted down into a frown.

"Yes." I had wondered if we would talk about this at all.

"After my divorce is final, I want you to come back."

My mind stuttered to a stop. "What did you just say?"

But I heard him very clearly, and he knew that. He was frowning at me now. When his divorce was final? Those words changed everything. He was married. I had been sleeping with a married man this whole time. No, it was worse. I had fallen in love with a married man. Before this summer, I'd spent my life in my head. I always held back, but this one time I didn't. I let myself want more, and this was where it took me?

"You didn't tell me you were still married." My voice was low as I tried to contain the emotions that threatened to pour out of me.

"I thought you knew," he said slowly. "I mean, you expected Rebecca to be here when you arrived. And our divorce would have been all over the news if it were finalized."

"I can't read the Swedish news," I snapped. "And on that first day you said…"

How did I miss this? I searched my short-circuiting brain for what he had said that first day. What words had he used that made me believe he was divorced? "You said there was no wife coming back."

We stared at each other, those words ringing in my ears. It had sounded just like "I have no wife" to me. I never would have slept with him if I had known this.

Are you sure? a voice whispered from somewhere deep inside. *Maybe you wanted this too badly to resist.*

I ignored this voice. I'd already told him about Brenda's married boyfriend one late night, about how hard this had been on our whole family, and never once did he raise the hypocrisy of our liaison.

"I'm so sorry, Ava. I didn't mean to deceive you." Edward reached for me, and I quickly moved away.

"Don't touch me."

The words came out sharp, and Edward's expression was horrified. He moved away. I quickly tugged on my clothes, trying to close off all instincts in my body that told me to give him a chance, to listen. I was having an affair with a married man. Just like my sister.

"Please, can we talk about this?" His voice was low and unsteady, and for the first time since we'd met, he sounded scared. Everything in me wanted to talk this out, but the fundamental truth of it was not going to change. Even if we talked about this, the thing that changed everything between us would still be true. He would still be married.

Tears welled in my eyes. I had to leave before I started crying, so I turned my back on the man I had fallen in love with and fled. I ran down the stairs, to the second floor, then continued to the front hall. I headed for the room where I had sat across from Edward that first day. No, that didn't help either. I needed to get out of this place, out from under the spell that pulled me to Edward. I flung open the back door open, letting in the storm. I ran, focusing on the cool earth under my feet. I had no idea where I was going. Not the cabin by the sea—that was Edward's domain—so I turned for the only other place I could think of. The forest.

The rain had subsided, but the wind whipped my hair against my face as I made my way across the cool, wet grass. I reached the path that I had walked just the other day, but it looked as though it had overgrown. Maybe it was the wind, blowing the branches across the opening, or maybe it was the forest itself, blocking my way. I heard Edward calling my name, his voice desperate, but I didn't look back. Instead, I started forward again, pushing the leaves out of my way. The forest was lush and dark and forbidding, the trees reaching for me, creaking in the wind. Pine needles poked at my bare feet, but I pushed forward, searching for somewhere to rest, somewhere to think. I spotted a large granite rock and headed for it. I curled up next to it, huddling, letting the night wash over me.

*

I didn't remember falling asleep, but I must have because when I opened my eyes, there was a blanket around my shoulders. What time was it? The forest was still, the way it was in the early twilight hours, no birds twittering, no chipmunks scurrying through the underbrush. The storm had blown over, and a thick fog had settled into the trees. I pushed myself to standing, my rear and my legs aching from the cold, hard stone.

I needed to get back to the house. It was my last day with Sofia. No matter how hurt and angry I was with Edward, I cared about Sofia too much not to be there for her. I had to put my feelings for Edward aside.

I crept into the house and headed for the staircase, but there was a dim light glowing from the library. I slowed to a stop next to the doorway, took a breath, and peeked in. Edward was asleep in the armchair I'd found him in that first morning, and he looked like the man who'd answered the door the first day. His hair was a mess and his shirt was wrinkled, the shirt tails were untucked. He was disheveled in a way I assumed meant he'd been drinking, though I didn't see the empty glass nor the bottle on the mahogany table next to him.

Something twisted deep in my stomach, and I had to look away. Just seeing him hurt. I turned away and ran up the stairs and into my bedroom. I stood in my shower, trying to wash away all the pain from the night. It didn't help. I lay in bed awake as the night turned to day, listening to the wind, counting the hours until I left. When I grew too restless, I snuck downstairs, into Rebecca's study. I lingered at her desk, taking one last look at the photos, then grabbed a handful of envelopes and left.

Sofia and I spent the morning getting my belongings ready.

"Promise you'll write to me?" she asked.

“I promise.” I dug around in my purse and found the envelopes I had taken from Rebecca’s desk. “These are addressed to me. If you want to draw me a picture or tell me about your day, you can use them.”

She gave me a sad smile, and in that moment she looked so much like Edward that it hurt. I open my arms, and she came to me, hugging me.

“I’ll miss you, Sofia,” I whispered.

“Me too.”

A taxi was supposed to pick me up at noon. Britt-Marie glanced at me as I passed her in the kitchen with a satisfied smile. There was no way she could know what had passed between Edward and me the night before, but my mood was probably enough to convey that I was leaving the Vallenberg house for good.

Sofia and Edward waited in the front hallway to see me off.

Sofia squeezed me tightly and let me go. Her gaze stayed on me, and I wondered if it was wise to even touch Edward. Finally, I reached out my hand for a handshake and braced myself. It didn’t matter. Just the touch of his hand on mine shot flames through my body, so I gave into that feeling one last time. Gently, he tugged my hand, pulling me closer.

“Please don’t go.” His voice was barely there, too soft for Sofia to hear. “Please stay. Don’t leave like this.”

A lump was rising in my throat, and I took an unsteady breath. If I looked up at him right now, I knew

I wouldn't have the strength to say what I needed to say. Instead, I closed my eyes. "Don't contact me."

Then I turned my back to him and walked out the door, the scent of roses following me to the taxi.

*

The plane ride was long, and my sleep was restless and plagued with dreams of Edward, of the house, of the forest. That was better than when I was awake, wondering if Rebecca had come for Sofia, wondering if Edward was alone in his room, drinking. For once I looked forward to the subway ride home, just to be jolted out of my daze. Just days ago, I had marveled at how I had changed this summer, how I was finally living, not just dreaming. Now I wanted my old self back, the woman who could escape life and find happiness inside her head, but that version of me was gone. I couldn't go back.

When I finally stood outside my apartment door, nearly delirious with sleeplessness, the familiar worn wood and peeling paint welcomed me home. I had missed this place more than I expected. I turned the key and opened the door to find my mother, Brenda and Daisy all sitting around the kitchen table. Brenda's bleached-blond hair was tied into a ponytail, and she wore a white button-down, a short black skirt and black tights, her waitress uniform. Daisy's hair was wild and curly, the way she wore it when she didn't want to bother with the straightener. I always liked it better that way. And then there was my mother. She still looked far older than her fifty-two years, but she looked like she'd gotten a little more sleep over the summer. I blinked, a little stunned. They were all here, waiting for me?

Before I could take a step inside, my family jumped up and rushed to the door. My mother got to me first. She put her hands on my shoulders, assessing me, the way she had thousands of times before. But today, instead of pointing out something that was wrong with me, something I should fix, she simply said, "You're home."

That was enough for my tears to start falling again. I was always the sunny one, the reliable one, the one who smoothed things out, but for once, I couldn't hold it together. I began to cry.

"What happened?" my mother said quickly.

I tried to stop myself. I knew I shouldn't say anything, if for no other reason than I'd probably be violating my NDA, but I couldn't help it. I open my mouth, and everything came out.

Chapter 11

I kept my word to Sofia and wrote her letters. I told her about people I saw on the subway and what I ate for dinner, especially when I made something I knew she liked. I told her about the library near me, where I spent Saturday afternoons studying, and I wrote about the first snowfall.

Occasionally, I'd open our mailbox in the dark hallway of our building to find something from Sofia. I'd run my fingers over it, thinking about the way Edward must have touched it. I found myself hoping he had left a note in there. I wasn't even sure I wanted that, but the farther away I was from that summer, the less I thought about the hurt. If he had been any closer, I would have found an excuse to see him by now. Thank goodness he wasn't.

If there was any good that came out of last summer, it was that I was a whole lot less judgmental of

Brenda for holding onto hope for her married boyfriend to leave his wife. I hadn't made the same choice as she had, but sometimes I wished I had. A lot of times, actually.

I made it through my entire last year without a single professor crush, which was a record for me. I'd made an honest effort to turn my focus to Dr. Javier Flores, who led my senior seminar. He was a perfect choice, hot in that stern, exacting way I loved, but it didn't work. I seemed to be immune to my former kryptonite. This should have been good news.

I spent more time at Ruthie's apartment over the last year. Now that I no longer could lose myself in my fantasies, I wanted to get out. We went to parks and plays. Once she and I took the train all the way to Coney Island for rickety roller coaster rides and a walk on the beach. The warm sand under my feet was heavenly, but I spent too much of the afternoon taking long breaths of the salty air and thinking about Edward.

I also came to realize that though I missed my family last summer, I didn't miss New York. I didn't miss squeezing onto the subway or walking the crowded streets, nor did I miss the cramped room of our apartment I shared with Daisy. I missed the forest and the sea. I missed the salty air and the wind and the sound of rain on the windows of my own room. And I missed Edward. God, I missed him.

It didn't take long for Ruthie to catch on.

"Maybe you should just call him," she said. "You know, just talk to him. See how you feel."

We were over at her apartment, drinking iced rose tea. It was an unseasonably warm afternoon for May in New York, and she had opened all the windows in her apartment. The car engines and the voices and the stench of garbage all floated up from the street and into her tiny living room.

I dragged my feet up under me on the couch. What good would it do to call him?

"It's been ten months, Ruthie. We've both moved on."

She raised her eyebrows, and I looked away. Okay, maybe I hadn't quite moved on, but I should have.

"Something could have changed."

"I can't believe you of all people are encouraging me to check in on a married man to see if he's divorced his wife yet." She had been the loudest detractor for all my inappropriate crushes. "Remember when you told me, 'don't hold your breath for Dr. Chu'?"

Then again, Ruthie had gotten serious with her boyfriend David this last year, and it seemed to have softened her view that attraction and love should make sense.

Ruthie waved off my comment. "Those other times were different. First, this was an actual relationship. And second, from what you say, it seems like he genuinely thought you knew. I mean, he gets minus points for starting a thing with you before his divorce, but…" She shrugged. "I mean, they weren't together. She had moved out."

I frowned, and she put her hands up in surrender. "I know this is personal for you, and the married man thing has made Brenda's life really hard. But you're miserable without him."

I had gone over all these details hundreds of times since I had left Stockholm. I still hadn't gotten over the hurt. And even if I could get past it, who was I kidding? I didn't belong in that house, in that world, and he certainly didn't belong here in Brooklyn.

"It's completely unrealistic."

"Why?" She gave me a little shove. "You've been lovesick over a man for the last ten months, a man you explicitly told not to contact you. Ten months. And it hasn't gone away. So I want to hear all the reasons you shouldn't talk to him."

I sighed. I didn't want to have this conversation, but Ruthie wasn't going to let this go.

"You know the married man thing is a big deal for me, considering Brenda's position. And besides that…" This part was harder to put into words, but I took a deep breath and continued. "But what's the point? I mean, what would he want with me? I was the only woman around last summer, but he could choose anyone. There's a whole world he belongs to, full of wealthy and glamorous people."

I thought about those newspaper clippings Rebecca had kept, the black-tie events they attended.

"Sooner or later, he's going to walk back into that world. And I most definitely don't belong there. I don't even want to try."

Ruthie frowned, which was kind of a surprise. After all, she was the one for years who had talked about the questionable morality of the way wealthy people hoarded so much money.

"So basically, you're saying you're not good enough for him," she said flatly. "And this is because he's rich?"

I cringed. "I guess? Though it doesn't sound great when you put it like that."

Ruthie threw up her hands. "After all these years talking about this subject, I feel like you've missed a key point. Sure, rich people shouldn't hoard their wealth and are notoriously untrustworthy as a group, but the most important thing is that you shouldn't sell yourself short just because you don't have money. That's one of the very worst ideas in our society. You have to resist it. There's nothing better about being wealthy, and if Edward thinks there is, then he doesn't deserve you."

She looked more worked up than I had seen her in a long time. Then she blew out a breath. "But everything you've said suggested he fell in love with you, too. What if he believes that your background doesn't matter?"

I was trying to process what she said. Did I really think less of myself because of my family's lack of money?

Ruthie tilted her head and added, "I mean, what would you have said if I told you that I wasn't going on a second date with David because he didn't have a nice enough apartment or enough money to take me on a vacation to the Caribbean. As a bartender he might never make that kind of money."

I was beginning to see her point. "I would have told you that you're missing out on someone who makes you happy."

"I thought about how much money David made for a quick minute, you know," Ruthie said quietly.

I looked over at her in surprise. Ruthie looked away and tucked her hair behind her ears, the way she did when she was uncomfortable. It didn't happen often.

"Not that I really believe it should matter, but I was taught to think that way. Then I thought, *fuck that*. If I judge him by his bank account, then I'm not good enough for him. Who the hell wants to be with someone who believes things like that?" She shook her head, then added, "I feel the same way when you say you're not good enough."

I frowned. *Not good enough.* This was the wound inside me that never seemed to fully heal. Was I going to live my life in fear of it?

"But what about that house? I mean, it's gloomy. Maybe even haunted."

"I'm not suggesting you pack your bags and move to Sweden. I'm just thinking that you should call.

You never would have dreamed last summer would turn out that way. You have no idea what will happen."

I really didn't.

I swallowed and stood up. "I really should get going. I'm on dinner duty tonight."

But as I walked toward the door, she said, "If it's real, it will leave him just as vulnerable as it will leave you."

I thought about that on the subway ride home, and on all the other subway rides home that week. On Friday, I was still thinking about it as I walked up the steps of our apartment building. I let myself in and found my mother sitting at the kitchen table. She was staring at a stack of papers in front of her, and she didn't look up right away.

My mother was never home at this time. Her nanny job didn't end until after the kids ate dinner. I had a bad feeling about this.

"What's wrong?"

She looked up at me, like she was seeing me in a new light.

"Nothing's wrong," she said softly.

My mother, the most practical person I had ever met, the woman who had worked two jobs to make sure Brenda and I never missed a meal…she looked almost dreamy. Nothing about her life was dreamy. I racked my brain for what would make her look at me like this, and I came up with nothing.

"What's going on, Mama?" I asked warily.

She didn't answer, which made me even more nervous. She just stared at me, like she hadn't seen me in a long, long time. I had to admit it felt good. Since my father left, she rarely had the time or energy to see any of us. She was too busy taking care of all of us and holding herself together. But right now, she was looking at me the way she did when I was younger.

"Did you really love him?" she asked.

I hadn't spoken of Edward since the day I had come home. My family gingerly tiptoed around the subject the way we did after my father left. It was collective grief, an unspeakable hole in all of us, but what was done was done, and nothing anyone could say would change that. And yet, she picked up the conversation where we had left off ten months ago, as if he had been as much in her thoughts as he had been in mine.

"You still do love him." This time it wasn't a question.

I wasn't sure whether this was love or obsession or simply clinging to the past. All I know is that I wanted to see Edward so badly that it ached. "What's going on, Mama?"

"Sit down," she said, gesturing to my place at the table next to her.

I kicked off my shoes and sat, and when I did, she set an envelope in front of me. My name was on the front, written in handwriting I would never forget. Edward's handwriting.

"I imagined him like Brenda's man, but with money to smooth out the rough edges," she said, almost to herself. "But they're nothing alike."

It took a moment for her comment to fully register. Had my mother seen him? If she had, that meant he was in New York. My heart took off, so full with hope and wants.

"Did you talk to Edward? Did you meet him?"

My mother pushed the envelope toward me and tapped it. "He would like you to read this first."

I picked up the letter and ran my fingers over his blocky script, this tenuous connection between Edward and me. I knew I shouldn't be this happy to see it, but my heart was racing anyway. My hands shook as I tore the seal and pulled out two sheets of thick, white paper. I unfolded them, took a deep breath, and began to read.

Dear Ava,

Over the last year, I haven't contacted you. Frankly, it's been torturous, but since this was what you wanted, I held back. I can't hold back any longer. If you've decided you don't want to hear from me, I suppose you could have thrown this letter away without opening it. I really, really hope you haven't done that.

So much has changed, too much to write in this letter, so I'm writing about the things I think you would ask me first. I think you would ask about Sofia. She's doing very well. I started to read to her after you left, just the two of us, and that led to other games and walks in the forest. You should know our lives have changed significantly, and we have you to thank for that.

Another thing you might ask about is the drinking. That night, after you left, I sat in my room, feeling unable to face that night alone. But as I stared at my glass, I imagined what you were thinking. I imagined that, despite the way you left, you had sat on that plane hoping I wasn't drinking. I knew full well that you had walked out of here determined to forget me, but for that moment, I made myself believe that it would hurt you if I found myself at the bottom of another bottle, and that made drinking that night unbearable. That first night when you came to my bedroom, you suggested I find a reason to stop. I found one. There's more to quitting than this, of course, but it was my first step.

There's one more thing that you should know, something you probably would not ask me. Maybe you'd wonder, or maybe you've put this behind you. Still, I want you to know. Rebecca and my divorce is final. I don't presume that this changes anything between us. I wanted you to know I accept that it was selfish of me not to clarify this, not to think about how you might have viewed this situation. I am deeply sorry for this.

There are plenty more things, big things to tell you, but before this letter gets any longer, I want to tell you how much I miss you. I miss your brightness. Your curiosity. I miss the way you looked at the boats, at the water. How is it possible you only sailed with me once?

I regret all the afternoons you didn't come with Sofia and me.

I miss your voice too. Do you know how often I stood outside the door to Sofia's playroom, listening to you talk to her? I miss the way you talked to me too, the tremor in your voice as I undressed you, the things you whispered when we were alone. I'll stop here, in case your mother is reading this, too.

I can't tell you how difficult it has been to stay away. I miss you, Ava. The weeks I spent with you changed my life, and I want more time. More everything. If you ever decide that you want more, please tell me.

Edward

P.S. I met with your mother. I'm sure you'll hear about it soon.

I stared at the letter, trying to absorb everything he said. It was so open, so honest. He hadn't left me in his past. He ached for me, the way I ached for him.

"How is this connected to you, Mama?"

"Edward asked me to meet him and said he wanted to discuss a business deal. I was wary of the business deal part of it, but I wanted to give him a piece of my mind for the misery he put you through. So I met him at his lawyer's office."

Edward was really here in New York. The idea hit me again, more urgent this time.

"What did he say?"

"He said he had negotiated a price with the owner of our building to purchase it, and he wanted the new owner to be me."

Edward was buying our building for my mother? "What did you say?"

"I said it was a generous offer, but the building is old and needs a lot of repairs. And I certainly don't have the money for that." She paused. "He said that wasn't a problem. He'd set aside the money for renovations as well."

The shock was still in her voice, shock and something else. Then I finally understood what I had heard before when she spoke, the tone that I hadn't recognized. It was hope. I didn't know how to react. This would mean she wouldn't be working fifteen-hour days. For the first time since my father left, she would be able to make choices, real choices about her life.

"You said yes, right?"

She nodded. "You can have your own apartment in this building, and so can Brenda and Daisy. We could renovate the inside, one apartment at a time, and each time in a new one opened up we could allow tenants to move around."

It was as if a dam of my mother's pent-up wishes had opened. She could fix all the things the tenants had complained about over the years. These were the people that supported her during the worst times of our life, during those months when she couldn't get out of bed, when we would have been homeless if not for the help of our neighbors. She could give something to them.

Edward had given this to her, but I knew it was a gift to me, too. I no longer had to worry about my mother making it or my sister or my niece paying for college. I would have the freedom to choose my life in a way I'd never dreamed.

I moved my chair closer and kissed my mother on the cheek, then hugged her against me. She felt smaller, frailer than I remembered. "Congratulations. You're rich."

She laughed. *Laughed.* I had forgotten how much I loved that sound. "Not quite rich, but closer than I have ever dared to hope for."

Her smile faded. "I know there's a lot of things you need to consider, but he wouldn't do something like this if he didn't love you. It's really for you, you know."

I let her go, and she kissed my forehead. The strangest things were going through my mind now, like the fact that Ruthie had been right. I didn't believe he'd ever come for me because we didn't have money. He must have understood this dynamic because he'd just attempted to even the scales with his gift to my mother.

"I have his phone number," my mother said. She took a slip out of her pocket and set it in front of me.

I looked at the letter and the slip of paper. I needed to consider this carefully, didn't I? No rash decisions. That idea lasted for less than a minute.

I kissed my mother one more time and headed for my bedroom, closing the door behind me. Daisy wouldn't be home for another hour, so I took a deep breath and dialed Edward's number. It rang once, twice.

"Yes?" His voice was brusque, all business.

"This is Ava."

"Ava." There were so many little things I'd missed about him, but the way he said my name was on the top of that list. He said it so full of desire, with a hint of wonder, like I was the source of all his pleasure. Just being me was enough.

We were both quiet, as I adjusted to the fact that I was really talking to him again.

"I read your letter," I said tentatively, "more than once."

"I just thought you should know a few things."

Ruthie's words came back again. *If it's real, it will leave him just as vulnerable as it will leave you.* I had to believe this was real for him, too.

"I'd like to see you," I said.

"Tell me where and when."

Maybe I should have put off this decision when I wasn't so giddy with the thrill of talking to him again. But I couldn't. "Tonight at 8 o'clock. Night Owl Café on Flatbush Avenue."

"I'll be there."

Chapter 12

I fumbled through making dinner, and my absentmindedness led to an overcooked lasagna and a salad with too much dressing. My mother didn't notice. In fact, I'm pretty sure a hurricane could have blown through and she wouldn't have noticed. All she could talk about was the plans for the building. Brenda was another story.

"You've been holding out on us," she said as she cleared the dishes. "You look just as starry-eyed as Mama."

I bit my lip. "I'm meeting him tonight at eight."

I checked the clock on my phone for the thousandth time, then looked up at my sister, expecting reproach. After all the underhanded comments I'd made over the years about Donny, I was in the same place, unable to hold myself back the moment he rode into town.

My sister's expression was somewhere between smug and self-mocking. She blew a stray strand of blond hair off her face. "Donny can be an ass, but I love him. I'm trying to make the best of it."

"I think I get it." I still wasn't sure I would make the same decisions as she had, but I could see it was more complicated than I had initially thought.

"You're looking longingly at the door," she said with a little smile. "You might as well go."

I gave her a hug, a real one, and then I headed for the bedroom to change. What was the appropriate outfit for a sort-of date with the married man I had a fling with last summer? *Divorced*, I reminded myself. I searched through my closet, passing over my work clothes and the halter and short skirt I bought with Ruthie. No. I wanted something casual, something that felt…me. After going through the entire wardrobe, I went with the jeans and red flats I was already wearing and grabbed a white blouse with flowing sleeves. I twisted my hair into a messy bun and let a few strands fall free around my face. No make-up except for lip gloss, I decided.

I took the long way but still turned down the last block fifteen minutes early. I slowed my steps, hoping it would slow my heartbeat, but it didn't work. When I looked up, I spotted someone standing outside the café. He was tall, and his hair was a little shorter now, but he was dressed as I always thought of him, in one of those button-down shirts with the sleeves rolled up. His hands were in the pockets of his trousers, and he was leaning against the side of the building, like he wasn't in any hurry. Like he could stand there all day, waiting for me.

"Edward?"

He turned and pushed off the wall. His face lit up with a smile that made me breathless, like there was nothing in the world he'd rather see. He started toward me, and my heart leaped in my chest. I had to stop myself from running. When I reached him, I wanted to throw my arms around his neck. I wanted to feel his body against mine, but I resisted.

"Ava," he said in that low, husky voice.

I *had* to resist. It was just that his lips were so close. If I cupped his cheeks or wove my fingers into his hair, I could have urged him to close that space between us. My whole body ached for it…

"Maybe we should go inside," I said.

He looked down at me for another breath. That impenetrable gaze I remembered was gone, and his dark blue eyes were full of warmth and longing. When he took a step back and opened the door for me, I tried to ignore the disappointment. How would I make it through the evening without touching him?

The café glowed in the warm light of old-fashioned chandeliers, and candles flickered on every table. The quiet clink of silverware against flatware and the murmur of conversation surrounded us. It was a little strange. I had never seen Edward outside his house. We had stayed on his estate for the whole summer, and somewhere in my mind, I still thought of him as existing only there. But here he was, standing in my favorite Brooklyn café, looking perfectly at ease in my world.

"What would you like?" I asked. "I'm buying."

He didn't protest. "Thank you. A cup of coffee, please."

"You can find us a place to sit," I said, hoping a little distance would help. My heart was beating so hard, and I was having trouble not reaching for him, touching him somehow. The ache of the last ten months without him was almost too much to bear.

I ordered our coffees and searched for something New York-ish to eat, finally settling on a black-and-white cookie. I balanced the cups and plate, and I found him at a corner table, watching me. With anyone else, I would have looked away, but I was greedy. I didn't want to miss my chance to look at him. To remember us, just for a little while.

"I saw you graduated a few weeks ago," he said.

I raised my eyebrows. "Have you been cyber-stalking me?"

He gave me a stuffy, offended look, but then a smile tipped up at the edges of his mouth. "It was low-level stalking."

"Fair enough. I might have attempted to read more articles on you. I'm pretty sure the translation missed some stuff, but…" I tried to find a tactful way to phrase this. "You've led a charmed life."

Edward didn't smile. "You got to witness how I was making use of all those privileges."

It was a fair critique of his life, but it was a little harsh. He had experienced a tragedy that no amount of money could make better.

"Tell me about your year," he said.

So I entertained him with stories about my classes and the kids I had taken care of and the ways I had helped my mother with the building repairs. These were the kinds of things I would have been embarrassed to share last summer, but the more I thought about it, the less I want it to varnish over my life. This was me.

After a pause, I said, "Your letter was intense. And beautiful."

"I wanted you to know about those changes. But I should have laid everything out for you from the beginning. I was too focused on trying to resist…" His words trailed off, and his eyes narrowed, as if he was replaying scenes from last summer in detail.

I was too. The memories had dulled from overuse this last year, but with Edward here, the intensity of his attention on me, the images and sensations sparked back to life. But desire wasn't our hurdle. It never had been.

I looked down, into my coffee, trying to break the spell.

"You started something with me while you were still attached to Rebecca. I have my own trust issues. If…" It took a lot to say this next sentence. It took courage to presume this man might want something more than sex with me. That I was worth more. "If we were together and things got tough, how would I know you wouldn't move on and find someone else?"

He hung his head and closed his eyes, as if he could feel the weight of my worries. Finally, he looked up again, and his expression was serious.

"Nothing was unclear between Rebecca and me. We were over." He paused and swiped a hand over his face. "I can make promises, and I can try to show you every day this won't happen, but ultimately you have to decide if you're willing to try to trust me."

I looked into those deep blue eyes, and I found the person I was in love with.

Flawed. Real. Trying to be the best version of himself.

I took a deep breath and tried to open my heart. "I want to move past that, but I don't know if I can."

Edward nodded, his expression solemn.

"I'm glad about the drinking," I said.

"I'm seeing someone for it, too. It helps."

"How is Sofia?" I couldn't believe it had taken me this long to ask.

She had written me short letters, and her spelling was too good for me not to wonder if she had gotten help from Edward.

He smiled. "Good. Really good."

I wanted to touch him so badly. I put aside all my questions about the future, about what it would mean, and reached across the table. I let my hand drift down his cheek, down his neck, and he closed his eyes and let out the softest groan. I pulled away before I gave in to the temptation to do more. I searched for something else to say, to take my mind off his warm skin and the friction of his whiskers against my hands.

"I promised myself I wouldn't think about the future today," I said. "I promised myself I would just come and see what it's like between us."

He smiled a little. "How is it?"

"It's okay," I lied, but I couldn't help smiling. In all the relationships I had, romantic or otherwise, I was always holding back, keeping some part of me to myself. But right now, I didn't want to do that. Regardless of whether or not we had a future, I wanted him to know how I felt. "Actually, it feels really good."

His smile widened, and he nodded. "I have something for you."

"It's not an apartment building, is it?"

He chuckled. "Not even close."

He reached into his pocket and pulled out an envelope, placing it in front of me. "No obligation. You can toss it if you want."

Now I was really curious. I opened the envelope and unfolded the papers, scanning them. It was a voucher for a first-class, round-trip ticket to Stockholm. I swallowed. This was feeling like a lot more than a coffee date.

"Anytime you want to come, you can," he said, his eyes serious. "Even if it's just to see Sofia. Or just to fly away on another adventure. It's yours to do whatever you want. No expiration date."

I looked down at the ticket, then back up at him again.

"Anytime, Ava," he repeated softly.

Edward walked me back to our apartment building, and we took the long route, weaving through the neighborhood. But we couldn't walk all night, so I led us back to my front steps. I turned to him and swallowed back the urge to beg him to stay longer.

"I guess this is goodbye."

He nodded, but he didn't move. The pull was strong between us, so strong. I had promised myself that I wouldn't do anything rash today. But as I looked up into his eyes, so warm, I gave in. I put my hand behind his neck, pulling him closer. He smiled as my fingers threaded into his hair, and his eyes went half lidded.

"I've wanted to kiss you all night," Edward said, his voice rough.

His lips came down on mine, gentle, so achingly soft. A groan rose from him, as I opened for him. Oh, how I missed this. How many times this last year had I told myself it wouldn't be the same once we stepped out of the Vallenberg house? I'd told myself that this was all part of some charmed fantasy, much better in memory than in reality. How wrong I had been. This was better. Edward was opening himself to me, pouring every bit of himself into this kiss, and I was helpless but to do the same. I was falling again, falling so deeply, and I was tired of resisting. I had spent too many months trying to close down my heart to this man.

I wrapped my arms around his neck and pressed my body against his. His muscles tensed, and he let out something between a sigh and a groan as his teeth grazed my lip. I needed to find a way that I could kiss this man over and over again.

That thought was enough to make me pull my mouth away. He held me close, and I rested my head against his chest, listening to the pounding of his heart as I tried to calm my own.

"I promised myself I wouldn't get carried away," whispered Edward. "That I would give you space to do decide. That I wouldn't try to coax you."

He said it in that buttoned-up British accent, as if he hadn't just given me the most dirty, thorough kiss I had ever had. I smiled. "Is that what you call this? Coaxing?"

"That's the polite way to say it, I believe."

How did this man, so reserved, hit all the right notes for me? It seemed impossible, and yet all I wanted was Edward.

"It's taking all my strength not to beg you to get on a plane with me tomorrow," he said quietly.

My gaze didn't waver, and neither did his.

"I think you'd better go," I whispered. "Before I say yes."

That got a hint of a smile.

"I suppose that would be wise." He sounded doubtful, and he said it in that understated way of his, the way I loved so much. And here I was, thinking of the word love again.

Neither of us moved for another breath. He looked at me as if he was drinking me in, like it might be the last time we saw each other. Then he dropped his hand and said, "You know how to find me."

I didn't remember walking into the building or up the stairs, and I didn't remember sitting on the sofa, but that's where my sister found me that night when she and Daisy walked in. The door rattled and slammed, startling me out of my daze. Brenda stopped in front of me, looking down with a knowing smile.

"How was coffee with the man who broke your heart?"

Chapter 13

It was one thing to go on a coffee date with Edward in Brooklyn. It was another to fly across the Atlantic to surprise him. I was doing the latter, and even after an all-night flight, I still wasn't sure this was the right decision. Especially the surprise part. But I wanted to come when he was unprepared, just to see what I would find. I knew this was tied to my instinct to mistrust, but I couldn't tune out the part of my brain that whispered, *what if he hasn't stop drinking?* Or what if there was something else, something he didn't tell me about? Or someone else.

Of course, there were plenty of things he hadn't told me. We'd only known each other for a summer, and I hadn't told him my whole life story either. Still, as the taxi sped down the two-lane road that led to the Vallenberg estate, nervousness bubbled inside. I fiddled with the hem of my dress, trying to calm my restlessness, but the closer I came, the harder I was finding it to wait.

The taxi slowed and turned onto the familiar driveway, coming to a stop in front of the heavy black gates. I squinted out the window at the entrance in front of us. The mossy stone pillars and the forbidding wrought-iron gate look the same, but beyond them, the forest looked overgrown, the trees crowding into the one-lane driveway. Or maybe I just wasn't remembering this place clearly.

The taxi driver turned in his seat. "Are you sure this is the right address?"

"Yes?"

My answer came out more like a question than a statement, even though I was sure this was Edward's driveway. If I had any doubt, the house number was still etched into the tarnished plaque on the stone pillar I was staring at. Still, a wave of uncertainty passed over me.

"I'll get the gate," I said as I opened the car door. I wanted a moment alone to shake this ominous feeling I had each time I looked into the forest.

The driver said something I didn't catch as I close the door, and then it was quiet, just the hum of the motor and the rustle of the trees. A cool gust of wind blew past me. I looked up into the sky, at the gray clouds hovering, billowing, growing, blocking out more of the blue sky. I walked forward, small stones crunching under my feet as I stared into the trees. I'd told myself I must have imagined that feeling I got from the forest, as if it were a sentient force, but I hadn't imagined anything.

"This is just a visit, nothing more," I whispered, half to myself and half to the trees.

But as I reached for the handle, I saw what I had missed this whole time while I was staring out into the forest. The gate was chained shut, a heavy lock securing it. I touched the thick metal, cold under my fingers. I had a vision of Edward, struggling to break free of the past while the house conspired against him until…

I swallowed, trying to tamp down the panic that was rising in my chest. I couldn't let my imagination run down this path. I needed to talk to Edward.

I pulled my phone out of my coat pocket and found his number. The phone rang and rang until finally, *finally*, he picked up.

"Ava." Just this word, the way he seemed to worship my name, comforted me. I blew out a long, shuddering breath, trying to push out the chill of the forest air.

"Edward. Where are you?"

He gave what sounded like an amused little laugh. "I'm at home. Where are you?"

I stared out into the forest in front of me, dark and forbidding. The lock weighed heavy in my hand, cold and final. How could he laugh while he was inside this place?

"I'm in front of your gate," I said warily, "and there's a chain around it."

"You're here in Sweden?" His voice was full of surprise, full of emotion I couldn't understand without seeing him. The ache that had twisted inside me for too long gave a hard tug. "Oh, Ava."

"But—" I started.

He cut me off. "I don't live there anymore. I'll explain everything. I have so much to tell you, but first, I need to see you. Your taxi is still there, right?"

"Yes."

"I'll send you the address." He paused. "I want to keep you on the line and listen to your voice, but I need to leave now. If I'm not there when you arrive, please wait. I promise I'll be there for you."

"Okay." My voice was barely there, the shock of our conversation too much to process.

I hung up the phone and took one last look into the forest of the Vallenberg estate. Relief flowed through me as I climbed into the car and closed the door to the cold air. It had not swallowed him up or rung him dry of all the happiness. He had escaped.

I gave the driver the new address, and he backed out and continued down the road, taking me farther away from Stockholm. As I sat in the back seat, looking out into the trees, I thought about Edward's family estate and the dark forest that surrounded it. Had he moved away permanently or just for a few years, like when he went to England? What did one do with an enormous, empty house?

The taxi wound through the forest road, and then the road opened onto a tiny main street of a village. We passed two small blocks of storefronts with striped awnings, selling bathing suits, home décor, baked goods and other things I didn't catch. The driver stopped at the end of the street, in front of a long dock.

"This is the place?" I asked.

The driver showed me the map on his phone. This was definitely not a house, but I told myself to trust Edward. He would find me, even if I had somehow gotten this wrong. I could count on him. The taxi driver probably didn't want to wait, so I paid him and he drove away, leaving me alone. Though I wasn't completely alone. There were couples and families wandering on and off the dock and along the streets.

I rolled my suitcase over to an empty bench next to the dock, looking out at the sea. The moody clouds had broken up, and rays of sunlight sparkled over the water. Down the shore was a beach. It was too cold to swim, at least in my mind, but one intrepid girl with floaties around her arms looked like she was contemplating it anyway. A couple passed me carrying groceries onto the dock. They loaded them into their motorboat, then unwound the ropes and drove away. Shopping for groceries by boat? I wanted to do that.

Another boat pulled up to the dock, and it took a moment to see that Edward was driving it. He was wearing sunglasses and a T-shirt, but I recognized him right away. I grabbed my suitcase and started toward him, transfixed as he caught the dock with one hand, steadying the boat. He looped a rope over one of the metal T-like things on the wood, his biceps flexing with each movement. By the time he jumped out of the boat, I wasn't far, just a few yards away. He said nothing, just stayed there as I stopped in front of him. He took off his sunglasses, and I saw the intense blue of his eyes as his gaze met mine. He reached out his hand and touched my cheek, my neck, my shoulders, and then he pulled me against him. He held me, and I could've stayed like this forever, in his arms, the scent of him mixing with the scent of the sea.

"You're really here," he whispered in my ear.

"I am."

His lips were soft against mine, careful, as if he was testing whether this was real.

I didn't even know where to start with my questions. "Where do you live?"

"On an island out that way," he said, tilting his head toward the Baltic. "Are you ready to see it?"

I nodded. He helped me climb into the enormous speed boat, and we took off. The boat skimmed over the surface, and I didn't know where to look. At the endless rippling waves? At the sky, so large and free above us? Or maybe at the islands that we passed, the rocks and cliffs and houses painted in yellows and reds? All of this was captivating, but not nearly as captivating as Edward was. The motor was loud enough that it was hard to talk, but I was content just to watch him. His dark hair blew off his forehead in the wind, and a smile tugged at his lips as he looked out into the distance. He stood up at the wheel, one hand on the front window of the boat, his body at ease. *He* looked at ease, and now I was the one wondering if this was real.

We continued across the water, toward a larger island that rose up, tall above the sea, with plenty of trees and cliffs along the edges. We passed a long dock, the kind that could hold bigger boats, and continued around the island. The shore was peppered with brightly painted cabins and houses, with smaller docks sticking out into the sea. Then the buildings disappeared, and it was just cliffs and rocky shores. As we rounded the far side of the island, I spotted a dock, the wood bright, as if it had been built recently. Tied to it was the antique wooden sailboat Edward and Sofia had taken me out in last summer.

I glanced at him, and he gave me a little smile as he slowed the boat. More of the dock came into view, and then I spotted a barn-like building not far from the water. Was it Edward's workshop? Next to it was a long, sandy beach. The shore was protected by a natural inlet, and as we approached the dock, a house came into view from behind the trees. It was barn-shaped as well and painted yellow, with large windows lining the front, looking out at the sea. There was a small yard and a tree with a basket-style swing hanging from a long branch. The place wasn't large by Edward's standards, nothing near the size of the Vallenberg manor house, but it was definitely large by mine. It also looked a lot more like a home.

Edward slowed the boat to a putter until it was floating next to the dock. He tied it up, and I helped him put the bumpers out on the sides, the way I had last summer. He came up next to me, stopping so close I could hardly breathe. I couldn't read his expression until he pulled off his sunglasses. There were crinkles at the corners of his eyes. He looked happy, really happy.

"Welcome to my new home," he said.

"Where is Sofia?"

"With her mother. But she'll be here this weekend."

I'd been looking forward to seeing her after a year of exchanging letters, but I had to admit I was glad Edward and I had some time alone. Nothing between the two of us was certain. I had flown across the Atlantic after our first conversation in a year. Just being close to him was leaving me breathless, but the first-class plane ride, the deserted Vallenberg estate, this house on the island…so much of the world I had just walked into was foreign in every way.

Edward's gaze calmed my uneasy thoughts, intense, heated, and familiar. He cupped my cheek with his hand, and I closed my eyes, just feeling his touch. His lips brushed over mine, soft and salty and so very right. His tongue stroked mine, reminding me of all the nights in his bed. His kiss was a reminder of all the things we could be together, all the hopes I had tried to bury this last year. He kissed me like he was making up for every day we had missed together, and I told him with my lips how much I had ached for him. When he finally pulled back, I was dizzy.

"Britt-Marie is probably watching us from the window," I said.

He shook his head. "She doesn't work for me anymore. There's no one here except you and me."

I looked up at him in surprise. "No more housekeeper?"

He shook his head. "I gave her the money to retire early and said goodbye."

"Who takes care of the house?"

"I do."

"What about your family's house?" Even if he had closed it up again, the way he had all those years ago when he moved to England, someone needed to watch over it.

"That house isn't mine anymore. I gave it away."

"You *gave it away*?" I repeated, too stunned to say anything else. He not only parted with it permanently, but he didn't get anything in return.

"Who did you give it to?"

"A historical society was interested. I think they're going to make it into some sort of museum and park, but I'm not involved. All I told them was that I wanted to keep my great-grandfather's name attached to it."

"I see," I said, even though I didn't. Not really. Who gives away their family estate? I thought about Ruthie's indictments of wealthy people and wondered what she'd think of this turn of events. "That's quite a change."

"Living in that house meant trying to live by my family's expectations. Being the lone survivor has weighed heavily on me, and I've been trying to pay the debt I owed to my family. To be the man they'd want me to be. I was raising Sofia to be next in line. I was raising her the way I was raised. The way Rebecca and I had lived. But last summer, you gave me a taste of a different life. At first I thought it was just an escape from the past, but it was more."

This was the change I'd seen in him, the way his smile came so much more easily, the way he had looked so relaxed behind the wheel of his boat. I thought it was just being out at sea, but now I suspected it was more than that. Edward was trying to move on from the past that had weighed him down while also honor his great-grandfather. He was making peace with it.

"I no longer have the kind of wealth I did before," he added. "I've experienced so much pain and isolation since my family died, and I kept coming back to the question you asked me last summer. Did I want to live in the home my great-grandfather built, the one that was passed down from generation to generation? I'd never thought of it as a choice, just a duty. But you reminded me there were other choices. That I could have another life. And once I started thinking that way, I questioned everything. What would happen if I left behind more than just the house? Would I feel even freer?"

"So you bought my mother an apartment building," I whispered.

"There were other gifts to other places. Everyone I know thinks I'm making a big mistake."

He raised his eyebrows at me, like maybe I was thinking the same thing. I shook my head, but before I could find the words to tell him how I felt, he continued.

"I bought a flat in Stockholm for the winters, not far from where Rebecca lives, but other than that, this is what I have." He gestured to the house and the boat and the landscape that surrounded us. Then he looked back down at me with questions in his eyes. "I hope that doesn't change anything between us."

"I came for you, Edward. That's what I want." We stood in silence, the boat swaying underneath my feet, as I told him the truth of my statement with my eyes. He must have found what he was looking for because he smiled.

"I want to share what I have left with you," he said, his voice low, so full of emotion. "I want to start over with you, here in this house. I want to show you everything there is to love about the island and the boats, and I want to learn from you. I want to see how good we could be together when my past is no longer closing in on me. I'm in love with you, Ava. I was last summer, and it hasn't changed."

I swallowed back a lump in my throat.

He brushed his hand over my cheek. "Do you want to try this?"

"Yes, Edward. Yes, I do."

The boat rocked again, or maybe it was my whole world rocking under my feet.

"Then let's start right now."

He gave one more kiss and let me go. He set my suitcase on the dock and helped me out. I laced my hand with his, and we started toward the house, with my suitcase trailing behind Edward. We passed the sailboat we'd ridden on together once before, and I thought about all the afternoons we could spend on it in the future. We passed the beach, and I imagined Edward, Sofia and me digging in the sand and swimming in the cool water. We climbed the stairs and crossed the grass, and I imagined myself curled up in it with a book, reading all afternoon while Edward worked on his boat. Yes, I wanted this life with him.

He opened the front door and gestured for me to enter. The place was open and airy, with a wash of white over the wooden floors and walls. The furniture was understated, greys and whites, modern and comfortable, nothing like the rooms in his other house. A light breeze blew through the windows, and the linen curtains rustled.

"This is lovely," I said.

"There's a room down the hall that has the things from my past. But the rest of the house is new. I wanted a fresh start."

It had been almost a year since I had left him, but nothing between us felt awkward or strange. It felt magical, the way it had last summer, only this time, we were both exploring the magic together.

"Shall we begin christening the rooms?" I asked.

Edward looked down at me, the warmth in his gaze mixed with hunger. I stripped off my dress, my bra, my panties, and he tugged off his clothes, revealing the body I had missed so desperately. We were naked together again, and I reached for him. In that moment, I knew this wasn't just a visit. This was my life, my future. Our future together.

Epilogue
Reader, I married him

I fastened the clasp and looked into the mirror in the corner of our bedroom. The necklace was gorgeous, three diamonds set in a wispy knot of gold. Edward had probably spent far too much on it, at least by my standards, but I was trying not to think about that. Though he had given away most of his fortune, we were still more than comfortable. And I was still trying to balance the generosity of his gifts with my own instinct to hold back with money. This was likely going to be a lifelong project.

I smoothed the necklace over my collarbone and took a step back for one last look. My dress was white and simple, handmade and feather-light. It was loose but somehow also formfitting in the right way, with spaghetti straps and a hemline that grazed my knee. My sister had braided my hair into a crown around my head, and Sofia and Daisy had picked wildflowers from the forest behind the house early this morning and woven them into the braid. Ruthie had just touched up my lipstick before she disappeared into the bathroom. There was nothing left to do except walk down the stairs and out to the beach.

The cool sea breeze came through the French doors, moving the curtains and blowing the skirt of my dress against my body. I wanted to walk out of those doors and onto our balcony. I wanted to look down at the beach, where my mother, Brenda, Edward and a handful of other guests waited. Was my mother smiling right now? She smiled more often these days.

The wedding was supposed to start at noon, but it was currently 12:10 p.m. and we still hadn't walked down there. The truth was that I was nervous. Would something keep us apart? Would the Vallenberg manor house somehow reach across the Baltic to stop us? Or maybe the interruption would come from somewhere more mundane, like Edward's relatives.

I was curious whether any of Edward's family would come to our wedding. A good number of his relatives were still outraged that Edward had given away most of the Vallenberg family fortune.

As his uncle Stellan had put it, "If you don't want it, at least you should have kept it in the family. You owe that to your father."

I hadn't missed the fact that his uncle had written these words from his winter home on the Amalfi coast. No one in that family was in need.

Still, the comment had shaken Edward. I could tell the moment I had walked into his study. His voice was distant, as it had so often been two summers ago, back in that haunted manor house. So I brushed the hair off his forehead and kissed him.

"Family wounds fade, but they don't go away," I whispered.

When I thought about the past year, I wasn't sure I wanted my own family wounds to seal up and go away. They were what had brought Edward and me together, after all. Maybe it was enough to have someone know the wound is there, who understands that exposing it still hurts, even after all these years.

Edward didn't reply, but I could feel that he was listening.

"Sofia is your family too." I kissed him again. "And so am I."

A hint of a smile had returned to those beautiful lips, and he'd pulled me down onto his lap…

The door to the bathroom swung open, bringing me back to the present.

Ruthie smiled at my reflection. "Hey, beautiful. You didn't let Edward see you, did you?"

I shook my head. It had been her job to keep me away from him until the ceremony started. I thought the tradition of not seeing the groom on the wedding day was a little outdated, but if that summer at the Vallenberg manor taught me anything, it was that I shouldn't underestimate the power of things I didn't understand. Edward had had enough bad luck to last him a lifetime. I wasn't going to chance it.

Ruthie walked across the room and laced her fingers through mine.

"I'm ready for this wedding," I said, but my voice was tentative.

She gave my hand a squeeze. "Nothing's going to go wrong."

"I keep telling myself that."

We headed out into the hallway and downstairs. Daisy and Sofia sat on the floor in the living room in their pale blue dresses, holding Uno cards, but their attention was on us as we descended. Or, rather, their attention was on me.

"Oh, Ava," whispered Daisy. "That dress."

Sofia said nothing, but she came over and wrapped her arms around my waist. I pulled her against me, letting her feel my love for her, love that had grown this last year, as Edward and I tentatively began building a life together. We had both wanted to take it slowly, for us and also for Sofia. At first, I came for two-week intervals while she was with her mother. It had been painful to leave her two summers ago, and I didn't want either of us to get too attached before Edward and I were more stable. But after a few months of spending all my New York time longing for him, we gave up on the slow track, and I moved to Sweden. Since then, Sofia and my relationship had grown, and she had been the one to suggest she'd teach me Swedish.

"Är du redo?" I asked.

She looked up at me into my eyes and nodded, confirming that she was ready for the ceremony.

Daisy grabbed the two baskets full of wildflowers that we had all picked this morning, and she handed one to Sofia, then hugged me.

"Thank you for all the ways you've connected with Sofia," I whispered to her.

"You taught me everything I know."

My heart was soaring, so full as I thought about the way our families could be so different and yet fit together so well.

The living room clock chimed. It was 12:15 p.m., past time to begin.

I took a deep breath, the tangle of nerves and excitement and joy and love swirling inside me, threatening to burst me open. Outside, Edward was waiting for me. Edward, who was the center of all of this. So I took a deep breath and said, "Let's begin."

Sofia and Daisy opened the front door, and I watch them walk along the path in front of our house, past my favorite swing, past the tables, covered in white linens and set for the reception. As they disappeared down the slope toward the beach, Ruthie gave me one more quick hug. Then we headed out, her arm linked with mine.

The sea sparkled in front of us, and the islands dotted the horizon in the distance, their grey shores and green clumps of trees so different from the home I'd grown up in. Slowly, the beach came into view. The few rows of white chairs were full, and I spotted my mother and Brenda in the front. Beyond them stood the wooden arch that Edward had built, now woven with yellow and white and purple flowers, dancing in the breeze—my mother and Brenda's work. Edward stood under the arch. Once I caught sight of him, I couldn't look away. I had long ago resigned myself to the idea that I might never get over the wonder of this man. His hair had lightened in the sun this summer, and he had cut it on our last trip into the little village on the mainland. He was wearing a tuxedo, and my first thought was that he looked like the man I had seen in those photographs I had found in the drawers of Rebecca's study. But as I came closer and caught his expression, he looked almost…nervous?

I walked down the short aisle, the sand warm under my feet. There were people sitting in the chairs whom I didn't know, and my heart gave a little leap. Had a few of Edward's relatives come?

When we got to the front of the aisle, Ruthie gave me a hug and then sat down next to David. My mother stood up and gave me a long hug.

"You deserve all happiness in the world," she whispered in my ear. "I love you."

I swallowed back the tears that welled at my mother's words, open and affectionate in a way that she so rarely was. Then I let her go and walked up to Edward. His eyes met mine, searching them as if he was asking me all the questions that I had asked myself. Can a past full of sadness be fully mended? Will our happiness last? I didn't know the answers to either of these questions, but there was no one in the world that I would rather ask them with.

I took his hand, and he leaned down and brushed his lips against mine.

"You're late," he said. "I was worried you'd gotten cold feet."

I shook my head and smiled. "The only way off this island is a boat. If I were going to make a run for it, you would have noticed."

I was teasing him, but I understood what he meant. I also had been worried that something would go wrong.

The afternoon was a blur, with only moments that stuck out, dreamy and ethereal. The officiant was a childhood friend of Edward's, and he performed the ceremony in both Swedish and English. I'd been learning my part for months. Then Edward kissed me so thoroughly, as if he was just as hungry to claim our happiness as I was. Time seemed to bend every time his lips brushed against mine, the echoes of forever held in this moment.

We ate outdoors at tables set up with both traditional Swedish food and Italian recipes my mother had insisted on making herself throughout the week.

Two of Edward's cousins had, in fact, shown up with their families, and I listened as they spoke to my mother and sister in that same British English that Edward used. But as the evening turned to night and the caterers packed the tables and chairs and dishes onto boats, Sofia began to yawn. We called a water taxi for to take my mother, Brenda, Daisy and Sofia back to the seaside resort on the mainland. Tonight, the island was just for Edward and me.

We didn't speak as we watched the last boat drive away, and when I turned to him, he was looking down at me. All the questions in his eyes were gone, and in its place was tenderness and so much love.

"We're a family," I said.

He caressed my cheek. "How did I not understand that a family could be like this?"

Then, before I realized what he was doing, he slipped one arm under my knees and lifted me. He said nothing, just looked down at me with those dark blue eyes and then started toward the house. If I was heavy he didn't let on. He simply walked us into the house, kicking the door closed behind him. He headed up the stairs and into our bedroom, finally setting me on the edge of the bed. He slid off his jacket, and I watched, admiring the fit of his shirt across his chest. More clothes came off, and I was captivated by the way his bicep muscles moved. He had been out on the water quite a bit this summer, and his skin was golden under the crisp black and white of his tuxedo. I longed to touch him, but I waited. I wanted this to last.

When he had shed the last of his clothes, he turned up his hands to me. “I’m yours, Ava.”

I stood and lifted my dress over my head, letting it drop on the floor. His eyes narrowed, that familiar desire taking over. I unhooked my bra and tugged down my panties until I was naked, too. He walked toward me, like he was savoring these moments just as much as I was. He picked me up and squeeze me, his warm body pressing against mine, and when I met his gaze, he was smiling. Maybe even laughing.

“I have never been this happy,” he said. “I didn’t think it was possible, at least not for me. And I have never been so glad to be proven wrong.”

We stumbled onto the bed, laughing and kissing until the desire took over. He entered me, and I cupped his cheeks in my hands.

“You’re mine, Edward,” I whispered. “We can weather whatever the future brings. I know we can.”

*

THE END

About the Author

Rebecca Hunter is an award-winning author, reader, traveler, former English teacher, chocolate lover, and keeper of a very messy desk. She writes witty, sexy stories about complex characters and intriguing destinations. Her books have won the National Excellence in Romance Fiction Award (NERFA) and the HOLT Medallion contest, and her debut with the Harlequin Dare line earned a starred review from Library Journal. She is the 2021 winner of Romance Writers of America's VIVIAN Award in the Erotic Romance category.

For the latest news, free bonus stories and more, sign up for Rebecca's newsletter on her website:

www.rebeccahunterwriter.com

More books in the Nordic Nights series:
Stockholm Diaries, Caroline – Winner of the NERFA
Stockholm Diaries, Caroline 2
One More Night – Finalist for the Bookseller's Best Contest
Stockholm Diaries, Melanie

The Blackmore Inc. series:
Best Laid Plans – Winner of the HOLT Medallion and the NERFA
Playing with Fire
Baring It All
Hotter on Ice

The Fantasy Island series:
Pure Temptation
Pure Attraction
Pure Satisfaction – Winner of the VIVIAN Award

Made in the USA
Columbia, SC
11 April 2025